SPIDER
SPARROW

DICK KING-SMITH

SPIDER
SPARROW

...

illustrated by Peter Bailey

CROWN PUBLISHERS, INC. ♛ NEW YORK

Published by Crown Publishers, Inc., a division of Random House, Inc.,
201 East 50th Street, New York, New York 10022. Originally published as
The Crowstarver in Great Britain by Transworld Publishers Ltd in 1998.

CROWN and colophon are trademarks of Random House, Inc.

www.randomhouse.com/kids

Printed in the United States of America

Library of Congress Cataloging-in-Publication Data
King-Smith, Dick.
[Crowstarver] Spider Sparrow / Dick King-Smith ; illustrated by Peter Bailey.
— 1st American ed.
p. cm.
Summary: Spider, a baby abandoned on an English farm, grows up to be mentally
slower than other children but manifests a remarkable talent for communicating
with animals as he comes of age during World War II.
[1. Human-animal communication—Fiction. 2. Mentally handicapped—Fiction.
3. Farm life—England—Fiction. 4. World War, 1939–1945—England—
Fiction. 5. England—Fiction.] I. Bailey, Peter, ill. II. Title.
PZ7.K5893Sq   2000
[Fic]—dc21   99-30707
ISBN 0-517-80043-8 (trade)
ISBN 0-517-80044-6 (lib. bdg.)

January 2000
10 9 8 7 6 5 4 3 2 1

First American Edition

SPIDER
SPARROW

Glossary

blighty   a war wound serious enough to send a soldier home; also a term for England or back home

brush   the bushy tail of an animal, especially a fox

bully beef   corned beef

corn   the edible seed of certain cereal plants, such as wheat, oats, or barley

earth   the den of an animal

forward   advanced in pregnancy, as with farm animals

hacking   riding at an ordinary pace

holt   an otter's den

hurdle   temporary fencing

knacker's yard   slaughterhouse

RAF   Royal Air Force

ride to hounds   take part in fox hunting

sojers   soldiers

spinney   thicket

squaddies   soldiers

Yeomanry   British volunteer cavalry force, formed in 1761

CHAPTER ONE

INSIDE THE SHEPHERD'S hut, the only sounds were the chinking of small coals settling in the iron stove and the noisy sucking and occasional half-stifled bleats of a motherless lamb. The shepherd held the orphan upon his lap while he fed it from an old brown beer bottle with a nipple on the neck of it.

Outside, in the lambing pen, there was a constant medley of noise, the crying of lambs mingling with the guttural replies of the ewes, each in her straw-bedded square of hurdles. Accompanying all these sheep sounds was the sigh of the wind, a westerly wind that came over the shoulder of the Wiltshire downs and swooped low across the lambing field till it met, and bounded up over, the stout stone wall that protected the lambing pen.

Inside this, the ewes that had already given birth and those that the shepherd reckoned were close to their time lay warm and safeguarded from the west wind's buffeting.

The shepherd's hut was a shed-like building with a curved tin roof through which poked a smoking iron chimney and a small window, golden from the light of the storm lantern hung within. The hut was wheeled and shafted so that it could be drawn from place to place, and in it the shepherd snatched what sleep he could, lying on a rough wooden bunk.

The orphan lamb's needs satisfied, the man stretched himself out and closed his eyes, hopeful of a short nap before he must make his next round of the pens. Over his many years of shepherding he had trained himself to sleep for a quarter of an hour or so whenever he could, through the long nights at lambing time. Below the bunk his dog, a walleyed collie, blue merle in color, laid her head upon her paws.

Beside the lambing pen was a drove, a rough chalk track that carried all the farm traffic from the road in the valley right up onto the downs, and along this drove, a figure walked, striving against the wind. A full moon shone fitfully between scurrying clouds to show the figure to be that of a young woman carrying a bundle of some sort.

Coming level with the five-barred gate that gave into the lambing pen, she opened it, slipped through, and, after a gap of some minutes, came out again to turn back down the drove toward the valley road. Maybe it was the force of the wind, now at her back, but the girl's figure looked somehow dejected, head bowed, shoulders hunched, her crossed arms bearing no burden.

Inside his warm hut, Tom Sparrow the shepherd woke suddenly at the sound of his dog's whines. She stood at the hut door, tense and alert, and scratched at it with a forefoot.

"What's up, Molly?" said Tom. "Fox about, is there?" He rose and opened the door, and the dog ran out and along the line of hurdled pens to the far end, nearest the gate.

As he followed, lantern in hand, the shepherd suddenly heard, amid the high cries of lambs and the deep, comforting bleats of ewes, another sound, a quite different sound—a thin wailing. He began to run toward the last pen in the line, beside which Molly stood waiting and wagging.

On Tom's previous rounds, this pen had been empty. Now, as he raised the lantern high, he could see, lying in the bed of wheat straw, what looked like a small bundle of some kind of clothing. It was an old, once-white woolen shawl, the shepherd could see, and from it came the feeble wailing, and within it, he found as he parted it, was a very young baby.

Quickly Tom picked up the bundle, carried it back to his hut, and laid it in a sack-lined box by the side of the orphan lamb, while he poured milk into an old tin saucepan and put it on top of the stove to heat.

Then, sitting close beside the warmth, he unwrapped the still-wailing baby and laid it across his lap, to examine it, as any good stockman inspects any newborn creature — to note its sex and its state of health, and generally to determine whether it is strong or weak, normal or malformed.

Inside the shawl, the shepherd noticed, was a crumpled sheet of paper. He picked it up and saw, written on it in wavery capital letters, a message. He read this, and then he stuffed the paper into the pocket of his old brown dustcoat, belted around his middle by a length of binder twine.

The baby was a boy, Tom Sparrow could see, and very young, no more than a few days old, he thought. It was a long, thin baby, with none of the healthy pink roundness of a newborn.

Tom held it up before his face and shook his head. "You'm a poor little rat, you are, my lad," he said. "Bit of a young girl for a mother, I dessay, got pregnant by one of they sojers from the camp, I shouldn't be surprised, and never dared to tell her family. And now she's ditched you. We'll have to try and find her, but first we got to keep you alive."

At the sight of the bottle, filled with warm milk, the orphan lamb began to bleat.

"Wait your turn," said the shepherd, and applied himself to the task of feeding the human baby. "Come on," he said, "get it down, you, there's a good boy."

Rather to his surprise, the long, thin baby reacted to this order as though it had been understood, and began to suck, gingerly at first and then greedily, at the rubber nipple on the neck of the old brown beer bottle held in Tom's right hand.

As he looked down on the baby cradled in the crook of his left arm, his own mouth began to move involuntarily at the sight of those little questioning lips, which had seemed bluish but now became pinker by the minute. The shepherd had no child of his own, much as he and his wife had wanted one. After fifteen years of marriage, they had given up hope of parenthood.

But every lambing season Tom, by virtue of his calling, found some unconscious solace in helping to bring into the world so many newcomers, and in saving others, like the lamb bleating in the box beside him, who might otherwise have died. Soon, as soon as one of his ewes dropped a stillborn lamb, he would skin it and fasten the pelt over the orphan, which the ewe, recognizing the smell of her own, would then adopt in place of her dead child. Not only death but the occasional dealing out of merciful death formed part of Tom Sparrow's life, and when a ewe was very old or sick beyond recovery, he would break her neck, with compassion but without fuss.

The essence of his trade, however, was birth, not death, and as he looked down at the sucking baby, he allowed himself a thought, which he then spoke aloud to the watching dog. "Ah, dear, Molly," said Tom. "I shoulda loved a son." Gently, tenderly, he touched the palm of one of the baby's hands with his little finger, dirty as it was and greasy from the ewes' fleeces, and the tiny fingers curled around one of his and grasped it.

Early on the next day, before the March sun had yet risen, Kathie Sparrow left her cottage at the road's side. In looks she was very much the archetypal countrywoman, sturdy, rosy-cheeked, clear-eyed. Oddly, as sometimes happens with man and wife, the Sparrows could have been taken for brother and sister. Each was of middle height, strong-looking, blue-eyed, fair-haired. Now Kathie began to walk up the drove toward the lambing field. She carried a basket in which was her husband's breakfast—bread and cheese and a thermos flask of sweet tea. There were bully-beef sandwiches, too—for his midday meal—and then later in the day, toward dusk, she would come again with his supper.

Each lambing season they lived apart, she in the cottage, he in the shepherd's hut, and for them both it was a lonely time, perhaps especially for her, with no child for company. All the other married workers on Outoverdown Farm—the foreman, the horseman, the poultryman, and three of the six farm laborers—had children of their own, as did the farmer himself. Although she was resigned to fate, sometimes Kathie could not stop herself from wishing that she and Tom had been blessed.

Now, as she walked up the drove in the growing light, she heard the noise of all the young life in the lambing pen, and she sighed. Oh, Tom, she said to herself as she climbed the little steps of the shepherd's hut and opened its door, and then, "Oh, Tom!" as she saw her husband sitting by his stove, a smile on his face, a sleeping baby in his arms.

Putting his hand into his pocket, he drew forth the piece of paper that had been in the shawl, smoothed it out, and gave it to his wife. "PLEASE SAVE THIS LAMB," she read.

CHAPTER TWO

BY THAT EVENING everyone on the farm—everyone in the village, indeed—knew that the Sparrows were looking after an abandoned baby, and a number of other people living in the valley had heard about it from the postman or the milkman. But no one had any clues as to the identity of the mother.

The popular view amongst these countryfolk was that she must be "one o' they girls from town, no better'n they should be," and that the father was probably, as Tom had thought, "one o' they squaddies." It was as though no local boys and girls could possibly be to blame for such a thing.

At five to seven the next morning, the farm foreman, Percy Pound, was waiting in the cart horse stables for the men to arrive for work. The carter, or horseman, as he liked to call himself, was already busy mucking out with brush and shovel and wheelbarrow. Some of the dung he would, by right, use upon his own garden. Two others, the poultryman and Tom Sparrow, never attended the foreman's giving out of the day's orders, for they were largely independent of him.

Now hooves rang hollowly on the cobbled floor as the horses shifted in their stalls, while Percy Pound waited for the arrival of the six farm laborers. He stood in his usual position, behind the big Shire mare Flower, his left arm flung up over her massive rump to ease the weight on one leg. In 1916, on the Somme, a German shell fragment had smashed his left knee, and even now, ten years later, the foreman suffered pain, pain that sometimes made him short-tempered, though he was by nature a kindly man. He pulled from his waistcoat pocket an old half-hunter watch and consulted it. As he did so, three men walked in together through the stable door.

"You'm late," growled Percy.

"Come day, go day, God send Sunday," said the oldest of the three, a small man with a squeaky voice. "If ever I do come through thisyer door of a morning, and you bain't led on old Flower's back-side, and your old watch bain't five minutes fast, then the natural world as we knows it will have come to an end."

The other two men, brothers by the names of Frank and Phil Butt, smiled at each other at these words. The speaker was their uncle, Billy Butt by name, and he never used one word where three would do, whereas they only spoke if they must.

"You'm late!" said Percy again, more sharply this time, as the last three members of his workforce came running in, jostling one another and giggling like the schoolboys they had not long since been.

One, a tall curly-haired lad, was Albie, son of Ephraim Stanhope the horseman. The other two were the sons of Stan Ogle the poultryman, whose love of chickens, alive or on his plate, was a long-standing local joke. Although he and his wife had given their boys perfectly good names, no one ever used them: Stan's favorite bird was the Rhode Island Red, and ever since his sons were quite small, the village had always called one Rhode and the other Red. Both, as it happened, had red hair. They were stocky, thickset boys, as like one another as twins, but easy for the village to tell apart since Rhode was shortsighted and wore spectacles. Now, at the foreman's sharp words, Albie, Rhode, and Red said with one voice, "Sorry, Mr. Pound," while looking anything but. Percy Pound gave out the day's jobs. The three Butts had to pull out and replace a long line of old fencing bordering a distant field. They were to load the fencing stakes, the rolls of barbed wire, and the tools they would need—crowbar and sledge, wire strainers, wire cutters, pliers, hammers, and a supply of staples and nails—onto the Scotch cart, and then Ephraim would drive them and their materials up the drove to the downs.

Rhode and Red were to go thistle cutting in a piece of rough ground. "And I'll be up later on," said the foreman, "and if I see one single thistle or nettle or dock as you've missed, you'm in trouble. As for you, Albie, I want you to go up to the lambing pen and give Tom a hand. He's been a bit busy lately, one way or another."

"I bin on this farm fifty year, man and boy," squeaked Billy Butt, "and I never heerd tell o' such a thing. Boy-child it is, my missus says. 'Poor little bastard,' I says to her. 'Billy,' she says, 'your language!' 'Well, that's what he is, thee'st know,' I says, 'a bastard, no messin.' Call a spade a spade, I says. What d'you reckon will happen to un, Percy? Will Tom and Kathie be let keep un?"

"Depends," said the foreman. "The mother might come back and claim him, I suppose."

Frank and Phil Butt shook their heads. "Never," they said.

"Does Mister know about all this?" said Ephraim the horseman, leaning on his yard brush.

"Mister" was how all the workers referred to their employer. Major Yorke was what was known as a gentleman farmer, an appellation to which he took no exception. This meant, in effect, that, unlike his men, he had no need to get his hands or his boots dirty, though he liked to put in some time at haymaking, driving about the fields in an impressive old Lea-Francis open tourer on the front of which was fixed a hay sweep.

He had been a regular soldier but had left the army on inheriting the farm from a relative. He loved above all things to ride to hounds.

"Yes," said Percy in answer to the horseman's question. "He knows. 'Twill all have to go through the proper channels, of course, but if Tom and Kathie decide to adopt the babbie, well, good luck to 'em, Mister said."

Percy Pound and Major Yorke might almost have belonged to separate species, so different were their lifestyles, but Percy respected his employer simply because they alone had been through the Great War. Billy and Ephraim and Stan had been too old, Frank and Phil too young, and as for the other three, they had hardly been born when the armistice was signed. Tom had joined up, but the Great War ended before he had seen action.

"What they going to call the baby, Mr. Pound?" asked Albie Stanhope.

"I got no idea, boy," growled the foreman (thinking about the war had made his knee ache), "but I know what I'm going to call you if you don't get to work. Go on, off you go, and you two, Rhode and Red, don't forget to take a whetstone. You can't cut thistles with a blunt sickle."

Later, while the fencing party was loading the Scotch cart, Percy walked with his distinctive limp, for his left knee was locked stiff, out of the farm-yard and up the road to the Sparrows' cottage. He knocked on the door with his stick, and Kathie came to it, carrying the baby.

"Morning, Kath," said the foreman. "How's it going, then? Anything we can do to help?"

"It's all right, thanks, Percy," Kathie said.

The foreman looked carefully into the face of the foundling. No beauty, he thought, and he doesn't look strong.

"He's beautiful, isn't he?" said Kathie.

"What you going to call him, then?"

"Well," said Kathie, "Tom wants to call him John after his old dad and I want to call him Joe after mine."

"You'll have to toss for it, then."

"Don't know as we'll be let keep him," said the shepherd's wife. "After all, 'tisn't as though he was a normal baby."

"Not normal?" said Percy. "What d'you mean?"

"I mean we don't know who he belongs to."

CHAPTER THREE

MORE THAN TWO years later, John Joseph Sparrow was moving rapidly across the postage stamp–sized lawn at the rear of the shepherd's cottage. Kathie and Tom worried a little bit that the boy showed no signs of walking, but he got about well enough, using his own peculiar method. It could hardly be called a crawl, because his knees did not touch the ground, but on what seemed like unusually long arms and legs, he scurried about on hands and feet—like a spider.

Kathie Sparrow watched him fondly from her back door. Our little Spider, she said to herself, for that was their nickname for the child that they had finally been able formally to adopt. This had been due in some measure, it seemed, to Mister's influence, for Major Yorke was a magistrate and a power in the district.

"Spider!" she called now, and the little boy came scuttling back across the grass toward her. He sat up on his thin backside and stared up at her, smiling a lopsided smile.

"Who's a good boy, then?" said Kathie, and Spider, prodding himself in the chest with a forefinger, replied, "Good un!" At almost two and a half these were the only intelligible sounds he had thus far uttered, and about this absence of speech Kathie and Tom worried a great deal. Each wanted to ask the other the same question, yet each refrained from doing so. Is this a normal child? each parent thought.

In the village there was little doubt. Other mothers, meeting Kathie with her baby in his baby carriage, at the market, at the post office, at the baker's, had from the start taken a kindly interest in the foundling, and had at first thought him an ordinary, if somewhat strange-looking, infant. But as time passed, their suspicions grew, and now they spoke of them to each other and to their husbands.

"Wass think of thik baby of Kath Sparrow's, then?" would be an opening question, and the replies would be varied yet similar.

"Funny little chap, ain't he?"

"Got a funny look about him, thee'st know."

"Seems a bit slow."

"Don't say much."

"I'd worry if I was Kath."

No one said, as they said of their own and others' children, "He's lovely, isn't he!"

Everyone thought—some with pity, some without—that it rather looked as if John Joseph Sparrow, known by now to all as Spider, was different.

Betty Ogle, the poultryman's wife, sharp-eyed and blunt-spoken, summed it up one Sunday morning as she came out of church (despite having just listened to the vicar's sermon, which took as its text St. Matthew's dictum "Thou shalt love thy neighbor as thyself"). "Tom and Kath Sparrow's baby?" she said to a group of others as they walked down the churchyard path. "I'll tell you what I think. He's queer in the head. They've only got themselves to blame. Same as I said to Stan at the time, they'd have been better letting the child be took to the orphanage."

On the evening of that same Sunday, a fine summer's evening, Tom Sparrow was hoeing weeds in his cabbage patch when his wife came down the garden path, Spider in her arms.

"It's time for his bed," she said. "Say good night to your dad, Spider."

Spider grinned. "Good un!" he said.

"You and your 'good un,'" said Kathie. "Say good night, there's a good boy." But the child only pointed to himself and repeated his catch phrase.

"Sleep well, my son," said Tom. "Pleasant dreams."

"I suppose he does dream?" said Kathie. "He sleeps so sound. I don't think he's ever woke us."

"He's contented, that's why," said Tom. I hope, he thought as he watched them go back up the path to the cottage. I hope he's content, poor little chap, because of one thing I'm certain now—he's simple. I don't know how Kath will take it when she realizes.

Upstairs, Kathie tucked Spider up in bed. She bent to kiss him, and he smiled his twisted smile and then shut his eyes as though he would be asleep in an instant.

Which he will be, thought Kathie as she left the room. He don't never complain nor grizzle like most babies do, some time or another. Don't cry much neither, hardly ever heard him cry. Yet when I come in in the morning, he'll be lying there with his eyes wide open just as if he'd been awake all night. He's not like a normal baby.

Suddenly, at this last thought, a suspicion that Kathie Sparrow had harbored for some time but had suppressed became a certainty. "He's *not* a normal baby," she said quietly to herself. "Thank the Lord Tom doesn't realize."

That night she woke sometime in the small hours to hear an owl hooting. Beside her, Tom snored softly. The owl, she could hear, was on his usual perch, in the old Bramley apple tree at the bottom of the garden. She waited, half asleep again, for the bird to hoot once more, but when he did, it sounded much, much closer. It sounded, in fact, as though it came from the room next door. Spider's room.

CHAPTER FOUR

KATHIE LAY WIDE awake, tense, listening intently, but the night was silent again. She slipped out of bed, switched on the landing light, and peered around Spider's bedroom door. He lay still, eyes closed. I must have dreamed it, she thought.

The next morning she said nothing to Tom about the matter, but she could not get it out of her mind. Later, she was hanging out the washing on the clothesline when she saw a blue-gray bird fly low across the nearby field. Its flight was hawk-like, and it was being followed by a mob of small birds. As she walked back up the path carrying her clothes basket and peg bag, she heard the cuckoo begin calling from a little spinney at the bottom of the field.

The kitchen window looked out onto the back garden of the cottage, conveniently, in that Kathie could keep an eye on her child as he sat on the little lawn or scuttled about it in his strange way.

Now, she saw, he was quite still, looking away from her, in the direction from which the cuckoo's calls were still coming. They ceased, but after a little while she heard a loud "Cuckoo!" from the lawn. Spider turned and saw her watching him.

"Cuckoo!" he cried again. It was a perfect imitation. Then he came scuttling toward her, sat beneath the open kitchen window, and cuckooed once more. He looked up at her, smiling. "Good un!" he said.

"It *was* you last night, then," said Kathie. "Oh, Spider, there's clever you are!"

Other children his age couldn't do that, she thought, copy the hoot of an owl and the call of a cuckoo—so exactly, too. Maybe I'm wrong, thinking he's not normal—maybe he's going to be cleverer than other children, it's just he's a bit slow learning to walk and talk. Maybe he'll not only catch them up, he'll pass them.

Later that morning Kathie heard a cat meowing. The Sparrows did not have a cat, but the Stanhopes, who lived in the next farm cottage along the road, had a big ginger tom, a ragged-eared, half-wild old creature that sometimes paid a visit. Kathie looked out now and there he was, sitting on the garden wall. She was looking directly at the cat when the next meow rang out, but his mouth had not moved. He was staring down at Spider below.

"Meow!" called Spider again. At this the tomcat leaped down from the wall and ran, tail held high, across the lawn, straight toward the child.

For a fraction of a second Kathie Sparrow felt a cold chill of fear, but before she could move a muscle, the cat reached Spider and proceeded to rub its big round head against his face, while he in turn clasped and stroked the animal. It was plain that they were the greatest of friends. Even from the kitchen window the tom's purrs could be plainly heard.

At the sight of the woman coming out of the cottage, the ginger cat, accustomed as he was to being chased out of other people's gardens, ran off and leaped the wall and was gone. Only the purring continued, once again, like the meow, a perfect imitation.

That evening Kathie could not keep this news to herself. Once the child had been put to bed, she told Tom—about the owl, about the cuckoo, about the cat. "I couldn't believe my ears," she said. "He had all those different sounds exactly."

"Well, I never!" said the shepherd. I'd sooner he started to talk, said some proper words, he thought. "He weren't afraid of thik old cat, then?" he said.

"Oh, no! He's ever so fond of animals, I'm sure. You've only got to see him with our Molly."

For ever since Spider had been a tiny baby, the collie had accorded him a special devotion. To be sure, she was first and foremost Tom's dog, to do his bidding and respect his wishes, but she seemed very attached to the child, lying by his cot when her duties permitted, and later, once he was mobile, delighting in being close to him and being touched and stroked by him. The touching and the stroking were always very gentle, and in return Molly would lick him as though he were her puppy.

"Just as well he is fond of animals," said Tom, "if he's going to work on the farm when he's older."

"He might not," Kathie said. "You never know, he might learn a trade, go to work in town perhaps. In three or four years he'll be going to school."

There was a short silence. Something told the shepherd that the moment had come when he no longer could or should continue this pretense. "Kath, love," he said. "I reckon 'tis time to stop beating about the bush. Let's be straight with one another, we always have. He's slow, our Spider, isn't he now?"

"He'll catch up," said Kathie hastily. "Look how clever he is, making all those noises."

"Now, Kath," said Tom gently, "I do know and you do know. I been saying it to myself for a long while now."

"Oh, Tom," said his wife. "So have I. He's not normal, is he?"

The shepherd shook his head. "What's the matter with him we shall never know, I don't suppose," he said. "Maybe it was something to do with his birthing or maybe it was the fault of his mother or his father, whoever they were. But we're his parents now and it's our job to look on the bright side. The boy may not look all that strong, but he's healthy, so far as we know, and he's happy."

"And you never know, Tom, we might be wrong!" cried Kathie. "We might be imagining it. After all, no one in the village has said anything to me about him, not even Betty Ogle. Have the farm men said anything to you?"

"No," said Tom. Not yet, he thought.

The next day he and Molly were up on the downs with the flock. The ewes were Border Leicesters, white-legged, white-faced, and imperiously Roman-nosed. Tom's critical gaze swept over them, elegant after shearing. With them was this year's crop of lambs, part grown now and showing by their coloring that they had been sired by the black-faced Suffolk rams.

Tom had the collie drive the flock slowly away as he looked intently for any signs of lameness or foot trouble. Then he gave the command "Away to me, Molly," and she ran right-handed around the flock, working them back toward him as he stood, leaning on his crook and looking again, this time at their forelegs. At the rear, one ewe, he saw, was hobbling, and, calling the dog around to hold them up, he pushed in among the mass. As the lame animal turned away, Tom slipped the head of his crook around one hind leg and made her prisoner.

While the rest stood watching, all staring wide-eyed at the man amid a loud chorus of bleats, Tom threw the ewe on her back and knelt across her.

A shepherd on wet land would have been confident of finding foot rot, but it was rare up here on the well-drained chalk, and sure enough what Tom found was a small sharp stone embedded between the clicks of one forefoot. As he pried it out with his knife, he saw a figure appear over the edge of the hill, a figure that, as the ewe had been, was limping.

Percy Pound liked to oversee the farm each day, and to this end he kept a powerful old motorcycle, which he rode along the drove. This ran, like a spine, up the center of the farm, from the water meadows that fringed the chalk stream at the bottom, past the lower flattish fields, and then up the steep ridge to the down above. Leaving his machine at an appropriate point, the foreman had then less walking to do in order to reach whichever men or whatever field he wished to visit.

"Morning, Tom," he said. "All right?"

"Yes, thanks, Percy," said Tom. He stood up to let the ewe free, and she ran back to join the flock, haltingly at first, and then, feeling her discomfort gone, more easily. "Picked up a stone," said Tom.

"Lambs look well," said Percy.

"Shoulda liked a few more twins," said Tom. "But it was a good lambing this year. I didn't lose many, nor ewes neither."

His thoughts jumped back to that other lambing time, when a newborn baby of a different sort had come into his life. Curiously, the same thoughts were going through the foreman's mind, for only a couple of hours earlier the subject had been raised in the stables.

Percy was about to speak when they heard a drumming of hooves and saw a rider in the distance, cantering toward them.

"Mister," said Percy. "I was just going to tell you he was on his way."

Major Yorke was a heavy man and it was a heavyweight hunter that he rode, a big bay gelding that he reined to a halt beside foreman and shepherd.

"Morning, sir," they said.

"Morning, Mr. Pound. Morning, Tom," he replied. "Lovely day." And then, even more curiously, he said to the shepherd, "By the way, Tom, I've been meaning to ask you. How's that little boy of yours getting along? I don't think I've set eyes on him since he was a baby. Running around now, I suppose?"

"He gets about," said Tom.

"And chattering away nineteen to the dozen, I daresay!"

To save a lie, Tom nodded. He caught Percy's eye and saw a half-wink.

Mister noticed nothing. "Good, good!" he said. "I must call in and take a look at him one of these days. What d'you call him? I forget."

"John Joseph, sir."

They talked sheep for a while, and then with a final word of farewell, Major Yorke clapped his heels against the bay horse's sides and away they went at a hand canter, over the springy downland turf.

Tom looked at Percy, mindful of that wink. The foreman looked back, remembering the conversation in the stables earlier that morning. He had given out his orders for the day, and one of the two Ogle boys, Red it was, had either not understood or perhaps purposely misunderstood what it was he had been told to do. Rhode took off his spectacles and wiped their lenses on a filthy handkerchief.

"Come on, Red," he said to his brother. "Don't be so daft. Anyone'd think you was soft in the head, like Tom Sparrow's kid."

"Who says he's soft in the head?" asked Albie Stanhope.

"Our mum do," said Rhode. "Going to be the village idiot, she do say," he added, and the three younger ones laughed.

Frank and Phil Butt reacted differently.

"'Tis a shame," said one.

"Poor little bagger," said the other.

Billy Butt, of course, had more to say. "Same as I told the missus," he squeaked. "Tom and Kathie'd have been better off without un. 'Twas a bad day for the Sparrows when thik babbie were dumped on them. Why, if that had been a lamb as wasn't right, born with a girt big head, say, and a girt tongue stickin' out of its mouth—like you do get a bulldog calf sometimes—or got five legs or summat, well, then, Tom would have knocked 'ee on the head, thee'st know. I bain't saying he shoulda done that to the babbie, but he ought to have let un fade away."

"Not for my money, Billy," said Ephraim the horseman. "I reckon Tom done right."

"And so do I," said Percy Pound, and his voice

was angry, "and I'm telling you all, here and now, you keep your mouths shut about that kid, especially you young uns. If I hear you've been poking fun so that Kath and Tom get to hear of it, you'll get your cards, understand?"

Now, as the sheep grazed peacefully away, Percy leaned on his stick and looked directly at the shepherd.

"He'll be all right, Tom," he said.

"Who will?"

"Your Spider."

Tom rubbed his chin. "You know, Percy, do you?" he said.

"Yes. We all know, barring Mister. All the village knows by now. Some'll be kind about it and some'll be cruel and some won't care—that's human nature for you. But I'll tell you one thing, Tom. Your Spider is a lucky little boy."

"Lucky?"

"Yes, to have you and Kath for his dad and mum. He's happy after all, isn't he, now?"

Tom nodded. But will he be happy when he's older, he thought, say in three or four years' time?

CHAPTER FIVE

THE YEARS PASSED and it was lambing time again on the farm. It was also John Joseph Sparrow's sixth birthday, so quickly does time fly.

There was, of course, no knowing the precise date on which he had been born, but Tom reckoned it as being a couple of days before that night when he had found the baby in the straw of the lambing pen.

One evening, as the light faded, Kathie and Spider walked up the drove to take the shepherd his supper. It was some time since Spider had graduated from his hands-and-feet scuttle to a walk, though his progress was not like other children's. He walked in a curious bent-forward manner, long arms hanging, and he was flatfooted, his feet splayed outward, each one planted deliberately as he went, as though he were crushing some creature at every step, something he would never deliberately have done.

The village boys copied his walk, and often, when Kathie went with him to the market or the post office, there would be two or three children behind them, aping Spider's gait. If Kathie looked around, the boys would instantly revert to a normal walk, giggling and sniggering.

Among the adult villagers, the reactions to Spider as the years passed were as Percy Pound had forecast. Some took little or no notice of the boy, while others showed, by remarks passed or by the mere expression on their faces, that they found the child in some degree repellent. But there were still plenty who would trouble to speak a kind word.

"My, you've grown, Spider!" they might say, and Spider, smiling, would reply, "Good un!"

But these were no longer his only words. A stranger listening to the boy talking would realize immediately—as everyone in the village did—that this was no ordinary child. But all the same Spider now had a rudimentary vocabulary of his own. Tom was "Dada," and Kathie was "Mum," and he used a number of other words, chiefly the names of the creatures around him. "Molly" had been the first new word that he had spoken, and, appropriately, "sheep" and "lamb" soon followed.

Tom and Kathie played on his interest in animals and would repeat their names to him. Once he had connected name and creature, he never forgot them, though sometimes his version differed from the normal. A blackbird, for example, was a "birdblack," a crow was a "croak," and rabbits were "barrits," but one name he always pronounced correctly was "sparrow." He knew his own name now, though this in itself was a little confusing for him, so that sometimes he called sparrows spiders and sometimes he would come upon a spider and say, "Sparrow!"

Now, as he walked up the drove with his mother, a large flock of lapwings, or green plovers, that had been standing in a field rose as one and lifted away with mournful cries. Spider knew them by the name that was locally used, and he pointed and cried, "Peewit! Peewit!"

They reached the lambing pens just in time to see the shepherd in the act of drawing a lamb from a ewe. He was holding the baby's forelegs, and he pulled, gently but strongly, in concert with the mother's contractions, till, with a slippery run, out upon the wet straw came the newborn lamb, limp and wet and stained with birth fluid. Quickly Tom cleared its mouth and pumped its forelegs around till he was satisfied that it was taking its first gulps of air. Then he placed the lamb by the head of the ewe and she began to lick it.

"He's a big one, isn't he, Tom?" Kathie said.

"He is," said Tom, "and awkward, too. He had his head turned back and I had a bit of a job with him. Just as well there wasn't a twin behind him or it might have been trouble."

Spider was watching the ewe as she worked on the lamb, bleating softly at it while it shook its head about and sneezed and struggled to rise. He pointed at it. "Good un, Dada," he said.

"You're right, Spider my son," said the shepherd. "Got the same birthday as you, too. Tell Dada how old you are today."

His age was one of the things Spider had learned over the past year. Now he grinned his lopsided grin and proudly held up his right hand, fingers and thumb extended.

"That's five, love," said Kathie. "That's what you were yesterday. Today you're six."

Spider looked from one to the other, puzzled.

"One more, son," said Tom, and he held up his own left thumb.

Spider copied him. Then he looked at his hands, at the four fingers and, now, the two thumbs. "Spider six?" he asked.

They nodded, smiling.

So Spider set off down the line of pens with his splayfooted walk. In some there were ewes with twins, in others one with a single lamb, while in two pens there were ewes that had not yet given birth, one actually straining in the first stage of labor. To each and all in turn the boy cried in a loud, excited voice, "Spider six!"

"Once lambing's done," said Tom, "we're going to have to see about getting him into school."

"If they'll have him," Kathie said.

"Mister might help," said Tom.

One day, admittedly a long time after Major Yorke had said that he would drop in and take a look at the shepherd's adopted son, he did so and realized immediately that the child was not normal. To Kathie, of course, he only said, "A dear little chap," but at home he said to his wife, "You remember that strange business a few years back when someone abandoned a newborn baby in the lambing pens, and then Tom and Kathie Sparrow took him on?"

"Of course I remember," she replied.

"Well, I've just seen the child and he's halfwitted, no doubt of it."

"Yes, I know," said Mrs. Yorke. "You must be the last person in the valley to know, I suppose because your head's always full of hounds and hunting. I've been to see him several times, poor little fellow. Of course he's retarded, but there's something rather taking about him."

"Jolly bad luck on the Sparrows," said Major Yorke.

"Maybe you can do something to help, later on, when the boy's older," his wife said. "Find something to do on the farm perhaps, something simple, just to keep him occupied."

"Huh!" said her husband. "He doesn't look strong enough to lift a sheaf of corn. Crowstarving's about all he'll be fit for by the look of him, walking up and down banging a sheet of tin with a stick to keep the birds off new-sown corn. Unless he improves a lot, which I don't see how he can, because he's never going to be fit to go to school."

On the morning after Spider's sixth birthday, Percy Pound had sent Albie Stanhope to give Tom a hand at the lambing pens. As Albie walked up the drove, he saw in the distance a horse and rider coming down toward him from the top lands of the farm. He quickened his pace and, when he reached the shepherd's hut, he called out, "Tom! Mister's coming!"

"Well, you'd better look busy, then, Albie lad," said Tom, who was eating his breakfast. "Start cleaning the pens."

But before Albie could begin, he heard the noise of hooves and then saw Mister dismounting.

"Here, Albie," Major Yorke called, "hold my

horse a minute, will you, while I have a word with Tom?"

The horseman's son obeyed with alacrity. He loved all horses, of whatever sort, and there was certainly an odd selection in the stables—the great Shire mare named Flower, several half-bred hairy-heeled cart horses, a couple of retired hunters used for light work, and even a large, shaggy pony called Pony.

But Mister's big bay Sturdiboy was an aristocrat of his kind, and Albie was only too happy to stand at his head and stroke his velvety muzzle and talk to him in that special way that people who are fond of horses do.

Inside the shepherd's hut there was an exchange of "Good morning"s and some general talk about the lambing, and then the farmer was about to leave again when Tom said, "Have you got a minute, sir?"

"Yes, certainly," said Mister.

"'Tis about Spider's schooling."

"Spider?"

"The boy, our boy."

"Of course, of course."

"See, he's just turned six, sir, and Kathie and me, we was wondering, could you have a word with the vicar"—it was a Church of England school—"and perhaps he could speak to the headmaster, to see whether he'd take the boy, this summer term coming. He's a bit slow, you see, sir, bit backward-like."

"I'll do what I can, Tom," said Major Yorke.

"Thank you, sir."

"And look here, when he's a bit older we'll find something for him to do on the farm. He could lend a hand in the season, for a start."

"He's fond of animals," said Tom.

"Good, good. Anyway I'll speak to the vicar."

Outside the gate of the lambing pen there was a short length of old walling, and by this Albie Stanhope stood waiting, holding Sturdiboy. The bit of broken wall was of a height to serve as a mounting block, and, using it thus, the farmer hoisted his bulk into the saddle.

"Thanks, Albie," he said, and off he rode.

"He's a beauty, that horse," Albie said to Tom as he went to fetch wheelbarrow and fork. "I'd love to have a ride on 'ee. All I ever gets to sit on is Pony—Father lets me have a go 'round the orchard when the foreman ain't looking."

"You might get your dad's job one day, when he retires," Tom said. Though my son, he thought, won't ever be offered my job.

Mister was as good as his word, and both he as a school governor and the vicar as another put the

case of Spider Sparrow to Mr. Pugh, the headmaster, with the result that, just before the end of
the spring term, Kathie received a summons to
bring her son in to the village school one afternoon.

As they arrived, the children were just coming
out to go home, the bigger ones by themselves, the
smaller with their mothers, and as they streamed
past, Kathie heard a lot of things said. Some were
good-natured, like "Hullo, Spider!" or "Good old
Spider!" but some children called out, "Good un!"
in mockery, and some, she could see, were imitating Spider's way of walking. Mercifully she did not
hear a comment from one of the bigger boys:
"'Ee'd have frightened Miss Muffet to death, 'ee
would!" he said amid the sniggers of his cronies.

Spider, she could see, was scared at the sight of
so many children and her heart bled for him. How
would he manage at school without her to protect
him? How would he stand up for himself? How,
with his limited and often strange speech, would he
make his needs known to the teachers?

One side of her wanted him to become a school-
boy, to learn, even if that learning was only to be of
the most basic kind—to write his name, to read a
few words, to know some numbers. The other side
of her half hoped, as they entered Mr. Pugh's office,
that the headmaster would not feel able to offer

him a place, so that he could stay at home with her, safe and protected.

In the end, it was no contest. Spider, already frightened by the crowd of children, now lost what wits he had. It mattered not that Mr. Pugh was a kindly, fatherly sort of man, anxious to put at ease this boy of whom he knew something from Major Yorke and the vicar. Spider simply clammed up.

"Now then, young man," said the headmaster, "let's see how much you know." He wrote in large capital letters on a piece of paper the word "cat."

"What does that say?" he asked Spider.

There was no answer.

Mr. Pugh pointed to each letter in turn, asking for their names, but Spider only looked up at his mother as though to say, "Take me away."

The headmaster opened a picture book, asking more questions about the illustrations but receiving no replies, except that when he showed a picture of a rabbit and asked what it was, Spider said in a small voice, "Barrit."

"Can he write his name, Mrs. Sparrow?" asked Mr. Pugh.

"No."

"Does he know any numbers?"

"He knows how old he is."

"How old are you, Spider?" said Mr. Pugh, but

even then in his confusion the boy only held up four fingers and a thumb.

"He's just six," Kathie said.

There was a silence while the headmaster looked at the little boy known as Spider and said to himself that there was no way such a child could be taught in his school.

Nervously Kathie said, "He's ever so clever in some ways, Mr. Pugh. He's wonderful with animals, any sort of animal, and he can copy the noises they make exactly."

"Mrs. Sparrow," said the headmaster, "it's better if I'm frank with you. Your boy has got problems that I don't think we can deal with. I'm sorry."

At these words Kathie suddenly and definitely felt not disappointment, but relief. She watched Spider's face as they walked home hand in hand, and the farther they got from the school and the nearer to the cottage, the more it brightened.

As they went in through the garden gate, he asked anxiously, "Spider not go school, Mum?"

Kathie shook her head.

He grinned hugely. "Good un!" he shouted.

CHAPTER SIX

THERE WAS NO dairy herd on Outoverdown Farm.
Instead, Mister brought in a large number of
stirks, that is to say, maiden heifers. These came
from Ireland and were all Dairy Shorthorns.
Though he knew he could rely upon the dealers to
find him decent stock, he went over himself, each
winter, ostensibly to check the quality of the animals on offer, but actually to get a week's hunting
with a well-known pack of fine Irish hounds.

The Shorthorn stirks were varied in color, red,
red-and-white, white, and roan, and Mister ran
them out on the downs, each bunch with its own
bull. Then, eight months to a year later, they would
go to Salisbury Market to be sold as springers—
heifers, that is—that were approaching their first
calving: "springing to calve," as the term was.

The bulls were all Aberdeen Angus, chosen for
their placidity but also because that breed tends to
sire smallish offspring, so that the Irish heifers
could calve more easily.

These cattle, a hundred to a hundred and fifty of them on the farm at any one time, were Percy Pound's special responsibility and interest. Of the other farm livestock, he well knew that he could entrust the care of the sheep to Tom Sparrow, of the horses to Ephraim Stanhope, and of the laying hens, which were also kept up on the downs in movable fold units, to Stan Ogle.

Of the other farm men, Albie helped his father or Tom as and when needed, and Red and Rhode Ogle gave their father a hand with the daily moving of the folds. The Butts, Billy and his nephews Frank and Phil, were general farm workers, able to turn their hands to any job.

The foreman liked nothing better than to ride his old Matchless 500cc motorcycle up the drove, or indeed across the fields, and then to dismount and walk across the down to check the cattle. He thought there was no finer sight to see than, against a backdrop of rolling downland, a big bunch of those Shorthorn heifers moving across the grass in all their variety of color, while with them, usually bringing up the rear on account of weight, short-ness of leg, and general idleness of disposition, slouched the stout figure of a bull, coal black and with not even the shortest of horns, for the Angus is a naturally hornless breed.

In the autumn Mister would often accompany his foreman on his rounds, so that between them they might pick out the most forward of the springers. Major Yorke was in the business of producing not milk but milkers, and it was Percy Pound's job to see that the springers left the farm in the best possible condition.

On a fine September morning in 1936, farmer and foreman walked among one of the current bunches of heifers. In some ways the two men were alike. As well as having both served in the Great War, they were the same age, and each had a family of a boy followed by two girls.

Physically, they were very different. Mister was a big man, tall and stout and red-faced, with fair wavy hair. Percy was a head shorter, prematurely gray-haired, lean of build, his face etched with lines that were the legacy of pain as well as age.

They looked at the cattle through somewhat different eyes. Major Yorke was a good judge of a horse or a hound, but he had come somewhat late to farming and lacked that stockman's instinct that his foreman possessed in full measure. Whether or not he would have admitted this, he was wise enough not to dispute the other's opinion of a beast.

"A nice bunch, these, Percy," he said.

In front of the other men Mister always addressed his foreman as "Mr. Pound," but it was "Percy" when they were on their own.

"And they're well forward, too," he added.

Percy nodded. "Bull's done his job, anyway," he said. "There was one or two as I was a bit doubtful about, but I reckon they're all in calf now."

As he spoke, the Angus bull sauntered by, his black coat gleaming in the sunshine. "Lucky old bagger, aren't you?" said Percy. "So many wives as Solomon." And the bull rolled an eye at him in passing, comically, as though he understood.

Master and man walked on across the down to look at the next group of springers, the farmer curbing his long strides to accommodate the limping pace of the other. The downland stretched away endlessly, the sky was as blue as a thrush's egg, and there was no sound but the singing of skylarks. No scene could have been more peaceful.

"I've been meaning to ask you, Percy," said Mister. "How's that boy of the Sparrows'? I haven't set eyes on him for a dog's age."

"Kathie keeps him tied tight to her apron strings these days," said Percy. "On account of some of the village boys."

"Tease him, do they? Call him names?"

"'Twas a bit more than that, back in the spring," Percy said. "There's a gang of them go 'round together, kids of twelve or thirteen, and they frightened the life out of Tom and Kathie's boy."

"How?" asked Mister. "What did they do?"

"They hunted him, sir," said Percy.

"Hunted him? What d'you mean?"

"Well, it seems that Spider had been out in the garden and I suppose Kathie wasn't keeping as sharp an eye on him as she did when he was little—he's ten now, after all—and she looked out and he'd gone. She went off down the village, thinking he might have gone there, but when she got back, she found him hiding under the kitchen table. Shaking like a leaf he was, Kath said, and his clothes all torn and dirty, and cow muck all over his face. She couldn't get anything out of him—all he could say was 'Bad boys! Bad boys!' A truck driver I met told me he'd seen this gang of kids out in the fields, didn't know who they were, of course, and he'd stopped his truck to watch. They were all chasing another kid. They must have come across Spider wandering about and thought they'd have a bit of fun with him. They were all barking like a pack of hounds and shouting 'Tallyho!' and 'Gone away!' and all that, and then they'd catch up with him—he can't run fast, Spider can't—and push him over and stand 'round him laughing, and some of them growling and pretending to tear at him."

"Like hounds with a fox!" said Mister.

"Yes, and then he'd get up and stumble away, the truck driver said, and they'd do it again. Till they got tired of it and left him, but not before they'd pushed his face in a cowpat."

"Wicked little devils!" said Mister.

"It's the same with animals, isn't it, sir?" said Percy. "They'll often turn on one of their own sort if it's weak or crippled."

This last word led the farmer to say, "Knee bothering you much these days, Percy?"

"No, sir," said Percy. "Not to speak of. Always better this sort of weather. It's cold and wet it doesn't like."

"How long is it now since you got your blighty?" Mister asked.

"Twenty years."

"I was one of the lucky ones. I never got a scratch."

"They're saying we might have to do it all over again," said Percy. "The way this Hitler bloke is going on."

"Except that it won't be us the next time," said Major Yorke. "It'll be our sons, your boy and my boy, they'll be just the right age, as we were, by the look of things. The Great War, they call our one. Wonder what they'll call the next one."

"You reckon it'll come, sir, do you?"

"Not yet awhile. But before we're much older, Percy, I fear it may."

"God forbid," said Percy.

"Let's hope He will."

CHAPTER SEVEN

BUT THAT HOPE was not to be fulfilled. Three years later, on September 3, 1939, Britain was forced, once more, to declare war upon Germany, and her young men, once more, took up arms.

The only sons of both farmer and foreman enlisted within the first few weeks, one in the RAF, one in the county regiment. The younger ones among the farm men were not called upon to join the forces. They, and all others like them, were deemed to be in a reserved occupation; they needed to stay where they were, to grow more food for their country. But the horseman's boy, Albie Stanhope, lost no time in joining the Yeomanry. (Little did he know that soon they would lose their precious horses and become mechanized.) There was thus one fewer pair of hands on Outoverdown Farm, which led to Major Yorke speaking to Percy Pound, and Percy having a word with Tom Sparrow.

One morning, after he had given out his orders in the cart horse stables, the foreman made his way to one of the lower fields, sown with turnips and thousand-headed kale, over which the shepherd was folding his flock.

As Percy approached, Molly gave one sharp bark but then, recognizing the scent and sight of the limping man, ran to him, tail wagging, ears flat back in pleasure at seeing this familiar friend. Once the two men had exchanged greetings, Percy said, "Your Spider, Tom. How old is he now?"

"Thirteen," said Tom. "Thirteen and a half."

"That's about what I thought. Strong lad, is he?"

Tom did not answer this directly. Spider, he knew, seemed to tire more easily than a boy of his age should. Instead, he said, "Well, he don't carry much flesh. Bit skinny-like. Why are you asking, Percy?"

"It's like this, Tom," said the foreman. "Mister don't want to take on another man in place of Albie just yet, but he said he could find something for your boy to do. If you and Kath were agreeable, that is. He'd give him a few bob every week."

"He couldn't do the sort of jobs Albie could," said Tom. "Not in a million years. He don't know nothing about farm work."

"But he could learn a bit, couldn't he?"

Tom sighed a deep sigh. "You do know as well as I do, Percy," he said, "that he ain't got a lot up top nor ever will have. The only thing he's good at is imitating the noises different animals make, and Mister ain't going to pay him for that."

"No, but he'll pay him for another sort of noise."

"Wass mean?"

"Well, there's all thisyer winter wheat that Mister's sowing, now there's a war on, and there'll be spring corn to come, too, and he isn't drilling it to feed the birds. *There's* something Spider could do, for a start."

"Crowstarving, you mean?" said Tom.

"He could do that, couldn't he?" said Percy. "Make a noise, shout and yell, bang on a bit of tin to keep the birds away? Or d'you think Kath wouldn't like the boy to be up on the farm on his own?"

"A few years ago she wouldn't," said Tom. "After those kids set on him that time, she watched him like a hawk. And he was scared for a while, wouldn't go anywhere. But he's got over it now and so's she, I reckon. I'll talk to her about it, Percy."

"Crowstarving?" said Kathie. "That's not much of a job, out in all winds and weathers, he'll catch his death of cold, and he'll be all on his own."

"He likes being on his own, Kath, you know that," said Tom, "and it'd keep him out from under your feet, and Mister'd pay him a little wage, Percy says. It'd be pocket money for him—you could buy him something down the market each week. I'd keep an eye on him, make sure he was all right, and so would the other chaps. He can't come to no harm, so long as you wrap him up warm, and 'tisn't as though it was hard work, just walking about, shouting and banging."

"To frighten the birds away?" said Kathie.

"Yes."

"Don't be daft, Tom. He won't ever do that. He loves the birds, Spider does, like all the other animals. You remember how he started off when he was little, imitating the owl and the cuckoo. Then as soon as he learned to whistle, it was the lot of 'em—blackbird, thrush, robin, chaffinch, woodpecker—he can do them all."

"Well, he won't be scaring *them*. Just the 'croaks,' as he calls them, and the rooks and the jackdaws."

"He'll never do it," Kathie said. "He'll let them eat all the corn they want."

The more Tom thought about this, the more he felt his wife might be right. And if Spider couldn't do a simple job like crowstarving, Mister wouldn't

bother about trying him at anything else, like helping at lambing, for instance.

But then the next day an idea struck him as he
was moving the hurdles to give the ewes a fresh bite
of the turnips and kale, and that evening he said to
his son, "Spider, how'd you like to work on the
farm, like Dada does?"

"Sheep?" said Spider.

"No, looking after the corn. Mister's growing
a lot of corn now on the farm, wheat it is, to make
bread to feed people on in the war, and Albie
Stanhope's gone off to be a sojer, so Mister needs
someone else to give a hand," said Tom. Though
the Lord alone knows how much of all that he un-
derstands, he thought.

Spider looked blank.

Nothing, thought Tom. Let's try again. "See
here, Spider my son," he said. "After the ground's
plowed and worked down and all ready for sowing
the corn, then along comes Frank Butt on the Fordson tractor and his brother Phil riding the seed drill,
and they puts the wheat in the ground. But then a
whole lot of birds come along and start to eat up the
wheat. Your job's going to be to frighten the birds
away. You don't have to hurt them, just scare them."

Spider frowned, looking unhappy. "Spider
frighten birds?" he said.

"Yes."

"Sparrows?"

"No."

"Birdblacks?"

"Well, these birds are black, but no, they're not the nice little birds we've got in the garden. These are croaks."

"Croaks bad?"

Sorry, all you rooks and jackdaws and crows, said Tom to himself, I'm going to blacken your names. And to Spider he said, "You remember that time when those boys pushed you over? In the cow muck?"

"Bad boys!" said Spider.

"Yes. Well, now, the croaks are bad birds, stealing Mister's corn, and he wants you to scare 'em off. You're going to be a kind of a sojer, like Albie. He's gone to fight the Germans and you've got to frighten the croaks, marching up and down, just like a sojer, and making a good old row so that the bad croaks all fly away."

Throughout this recital, Tom saw, the boy was becoming increasingly excited, hopping from one splayfoot to the other and swinging his arms up and down. Now he cried loudly, "Spider sojer?"

Tom nodded. "What d'you think?" he said.

"Good un!" shouted Spider.

CHAPTER EIGHT

THE FOLLOWING MONDAY was to be Spider's first day at work. It was quite a cold morning, and Kathie had sent him off properly dressed against the weather. He wore an old army overcoat that had belonged to Tom in his brief days of soldiering and was a good deal too big and long for his son. It reached down to Spider's ankles, and the waist had to be drawn in by a length of binder twine. In one pocket of this coat was a packet containing bread and cheese and in the other a bottle of cold tea.

He left the cottage with his father, and they parted at the bottom of the drove: Tom to go on up it to the shepherd's hut, Spider under orders to go down the road to the farmyard and report to Percy Pound.

"You just do as you're told, Spider lad," said Tom, "and you won't come to no harm."

Spider grinned and set off in his usual bent-forward flatfooted way, but though his feet turned as outward as ever, his arms, which normally hung by his sides, now swung vigorously in what he obviously considered a soldierly manner.

Ephraim Stanhope the horseman was always earliest in the stables, so that Percy Pound's first words on arrival were, as usual, "Morning, Eph."

"Morning, Percy."

"Dunno if I told you," said Percy, "but Tom Sparrow's boy's starting today. I'm going to take him up to Maggs' Corner, to keep the birds off. We drilled it with wheat last week."

"Oh, is that what he's on about?" said Ephraim. "'What you doing here?' I said to him, and he says, 'Croaks! Bad croaks!' and flaps his arms about."

"Oh, he's here already, is he?"

"Ar, and I'll tell you something for nothing, Percy, he's either fearless or foolish. He's been 'round all the horses already, talking to 'em, if you can call it talking, mumbling more like, and gentling them, and they've all stood there like lambs."

"Never!" said Percy.

"Some of them's quiet enough, as you know," said Ephraim, "but old Flower, she don't like kids anywhere near her as a rule, and Em'ly, she do lash out at strangers, and as for that Pony, he do bite— took a nip out of our Albie just afore he went off to the Yeomanry. But this Spider, he ain't afeard of any of them and they seem to know it."

Before Percy had time to comment on all this, the rest of the farm men came into the stables, first Red and Rhode Ogle and then the three Butts. Frank and Phil were biggish men, and between them their uncle looked even smaller than usual. Billy was approaching sixty-five now, but he could still do a good day's work, and, had there been a donkey on Outoverdown Farm, he would without doubt have talked the hind leg off it.

"Yur, 'tis brass monkey weather," he piped now, rubbing his hands together, and to the foreman, who stood leaning his left arm on Flower's rump as usual, he said, "I 'opes you got a nice warm job for me today, Percy. I ain't so young as I was."

"Go on, Billy," said Rhode Ogle. "You don't look a day over ninety."

"Shut thy trap, young Rhode!" squeaked Billy angrily. "Eighteen hundred and seventy-four I were born and that's a bleddy long time ago, I can tell 'ee. You wait till you gets to my age, which I don't never suppose you will, featherbrained young idjut, got no more sense than one of your dad's cockerels, and they don't wear no bleddy glasses what's more, chances are you'll fall off the top of a haymow and break your bleddy neck afore you'm much older and don't think old Billy'll come to your bleddy funeral, neither."

Percy opened his mouth to say, "That's enough," but before he could speak, Billy suddenly fell silent, for Spider had come down Flower's off side, from where he had been standing at her head, hidden from the men. Seeing Percy's attitude, he copied it. The mare turned her head at the touch of Spider's right arm on her rump, but then turned back, unconcerned, and pulled wisps of hay from her crib. The Butts and the Ogles gaped at this sight. They all knew that the Shire mare, though generally cooperative, had no liking for children and would shift about and stamp her great feet if one came near. Yet here she was, placid as an old sheep beside this odd-looking boy in the long over-coat. Even Billy lost his tongue.

"Right," said Percy Pound sharply (the east wind was making his knee hurt). "Perhaps now you'll let me get a word in edgewise, Billy. But first of all, this is Tom and Kathie's boy, as you all know, and he's starting work today, going to do a bit of crowstarving. Now, he's got his little problems, Spider has, and I don't want anyone poking fun at him just because he don't speak too well. Now then, Spider, you tell 'em what you're going to do today."

Spider looked around at the men confronting him and saw that each wore some sort of a smile, and he grinned back and said, "Spider scare croaks!"

"Good boy," said Percy. "Now you just wait awhile, and then I'll take you up to Maggs' Corner and start you off."

When he had given out his instructions to the other men and they had left the stables, Percy said to the horseman, "Got a bit of old tin about anywhere, Eph? Need summat for the boy to bang on."

Ephraim scratched his head awhile and then said, "There's that old broken swath-turner out in the backyard under they nettles. You could bash one of the wings off 'ee."

So it was that, ten minutes later, Percy Pound started up his old Matchless, on the luggage carrier of which he had strapped one of the wings of the swath-turner and a stout iron bar to act as a drumstick. He straddled the low saddle of the big machine, working the hand throttle so that the engine bellowed in short bursts, while Spider watched, jigging up and down in excitement at the noise.

Then Percy put a hand behind him and patted the seat. "Come on, Spider," he said.

Spider's mouth fell open. Plainly the thought that he was to be offered a ride had not entered his mind. He looked at Percy, he looked at the seat, he looked at the horseman, who was standing by, watching.

"Go on, lad," said Ephraim. "Jump on. Percy'll look after thee." And he helped the boy to swing a clumsy leg over while the foreman reached down either side to plant Spider's boots on the rear footrests.

"Now then, Spider," said Percy, "you put your arms 'round my middle and you hold on tight." And off they went.

Percy drove slowly out of the yard and up the road to the junction with the drove. Because its rammed chalk surface was rough, he did not increase his speed, but then they came to an opening that led into a large piece of permanent grass, beyond which lay the field called Maggs' Corner. Once on the grass and confident now that the ferocity of the grip around his waist meant Spider would not fall off, he moved through the gears until they were speeding along at a good rate.

Behind him he could hear Spider yelling, not with fear but with delight by the sound of it, and then in front of him he saw a black cloud of birds rise from the new-sown wheat at the sound of the motorcycle.

At the gateway into the field Percy switched off,

dismounted, and helped the boy down. He un-strapped the piece of tin and the iron rod from the luggage carrier.

"Quiet now," he said to Spider, and put a finger to his lips, and they stood still, waiting, while the birds circled above, and then, at first in ones and twos and then in numbers, flew down again and pitched farther down the field, in which the wheat was just beginning to show green in the drills.

Then Percy gave the rod and the tin to Spider.

"Now then, sojer," he said (for Tom had told him of his trick), "see all the bad birds down there, stealing Mister's corn?" He pointed, and Spider nodded. "Right then," said Percy. "Up and at 'em!" And he swung open the gate.

Then down Maggs' Corner marched the thin figure of Spider Sparrow in his overlarge overcoat, each foot turned out at forty-five degrees, banging his piece of tin for all he was worth.

"Geddoff, croaks! Bad croaks! Bad uns! Bad uns!" shouted the crowstarver.

CHAPTER NINE

CROWSTARVING WAS THE ideal job for Spider, though he could not have said why, even had he possessed the vocabulary to do so. To begin with, he was on his own, which he liked to be, yet never alone, for all around him were animals of one sort or another. There were the croaks, of course, keeping him on the move and requiring him to shout and bang his tin, both of which things he liked doing. But then in the quiet intervals, when the black thieves had temporarily left to pilfer someone else's corn, there were all sorts of creatures for him to enjoy watching. There were many other sorts of birds, some of which, like the wood pigeons, feasted on the sprouting wheat as greedily as had the crows and rooks and jackdaws, but because they were not croaks—and only croaks, he had been told, were bad—Spider allowed them to eat in peace.

At one end of Maggs' Corner (it was a roughly

triangular field) there was a small spinney of ash and hawthorn, and here the wood pigeons rested when their crops were full.

"Coo-coo-roo, coo-coo"—repeatedly they sang these five notes—and the birds soon grew used to hearing them echoed from below in an exact facsimile of their song.

The magpies, too, more inquisitive by nature, became accustomed to hearing, coming from the mouth of a human figure, their loud chattering: "Chak-chak-chak-chak!"

"Peewit!" cried Spider to the flocks of lapwings that flew over his head, sometimes with their peculiar slow flapping wingbeats, and sometimes throwing themselves wildly about in the air. And there were so many other birds, out there in the wide-open spaces under the huge bowl of the sky, that called to the crowstarver and were answered by him.

"Kiu! Kiu! Werro!" barked the little owl, abroad in daylight unlike the rest of his clan.

"Korrk-kok!" crowed the pheasant, and "Krric! Krric! Kar-wic!" grated the partridge, while high above, the skylarks poured down their long, drawn-out, high-pitched musical cadenzas. And all were faithfully answered by Spider.

In addition to these and many other kinds of birds, there were beasts on Outoverdown Farm:

rabbits galore, quite a few hares, and the occasional fox, hunting in the daytime.

All of these of course kept well clear of Spider while he was frightening the croaks, but in the quieter intervals of the day he had many creatures to look at. Sometimes they were at a distance, but, as though to compensate for his other deficiencies, his eyesight was exceptionally sharp and his hearing very keen. Some of these animals—like the "barrits"—Spider knew well, for he had so often seen them before, hopping about the headlands of the fields or popping into burrows at the edge of the drove, but he could not put a name to hare or to fox.

However, he had at home a picture book that Tom and Kathie had given him because of his interest in animals, and he would point out to them the likeness of some creature that he had seen and they would tell him its name (for he could not read a word). Thus, after seeing a hare lolloping across Maggs' Corner one day, he found it in his book, showed it to them, and said, "Big barrit?"

"No," they said. "Hare."

Spider looked puzzled. He put his hand up to his head and pulled at his forelock.

"No," said Kathie. "It's spelled different."

Not understanding, Spider said again, "Big barrit?"

Tom nodded. "All right," he said. "You call it that, son, if you like. We'll know what you mean."

Then, a day or two later, Spider saw a fox. He was sitting at the edge of the spinney, eating his lunch. Maggs' Corner was for the moment free of croaks, and only the privileged wood pigeons filled their crops. Suddenly they, too, all lifted off and flew hurriedly away, and Spider, looking in that direction, saw a red-coated, bushy-tailed figure trotting along the headland of the field toward him.

He sat quite still, even ceasing to chew, as the animal came nearer. Suddenly it saw him and stopped in its tracks, one forepaw raised.

Then a truly surprising thing happened. The fox came on, more slowly now, alert but showing no sign of fear, until it was no more than ten feet from the boy, and then it sat down facing him, ears pricked, eyes fixed upon him. It licked its lips. "Good un!" said Spider softly, and he broke off a bit of bread and awkwardly, for all his actions tended to be clumsy, tossed it toward this wild animal, which by all rights should have fled at the mere sight of him and would surely have done so from any other human being.

By some strange instinct, the fox seemed to know that this human was different from others and posed no sort of threat. It moved in a step or two and picked up the bread. It did not gulp it down or make off with it, as it would have done had danger threatened, but ate it delicately, like a cat. The bread finished, fox and boy remained quite still, each gazing into the other's eyes, and then, unhurriedly, the animal turned and trotted back in the direction from which it had come.

That night Spider got out his picture book and found a portrait of a fox. Excitedly, he showed it to his parents, grinning and pointing. "Spider see!" he said.

"Saw a fox, did you?" they said.

"Vox!" said Spider. "Vox! Good un!" and he pointed to his mouth and made chewing movements.

"Eating summat, was it?" asked Tom.

"Or was it when you were eating your lunch?" asked Kathie. To both questions Spider nodded vigorously, and then he performed a little pantomime for them.

First, he put a hand to a pocket, pretending to draw something out and break a piece off it. Then he carried one hand to his mouth and, breaking off another imaginary piece, stretched out his arm and offered it to Molly.

"Spider eat, vox eat," he said.

"Sharing his lunch with a fox?" said Kathie later when Spider had gone to bed. "Whoever heard tell of such a thing! Dunno what goes on inside his head."

"Dunno what Mister'd say if it was true!" said Tom. "Only good fox for him is a dead one."

"What does Mister say about Spider?" asked Kathie. "D'you reckon he thinks he's doing the job all right?"

"Too true," said Tom. "Couple of days after he'd started, I was feeding the rams in that long paddock by the roadside, you know, and I heard a clip-clop and Mister comes riding down the road, and he pulls Sturdiboy up and says to me, 'How's that boy of yours getting on, Tom? Mr. Pound tells me he's put him up on Maggs' Corner. Keeping the birds off, is he?'

"Well, before I could answer, our Spider starts up. Now, Maggs' Corner's a good half mile from the rams' paddock, I reckon, but you could hear him a-hollering and a-banging as though he was t'other side of the fence. And we looked up over that way and you could see a great cloud of birds lift off. And Mister looks at me and he grins and he says, 'He's doing all right, Tom. That row would wake the dead.'"

Spider spent a week or so more up at Maggs' Corner, by which time the wheat was up and growing well and the threat of bird damage had lessened, but on most of those days he came home and acted out his pantomime of feeding the "vox," so that any belief his parents might have had in this story waned and died, and they thought the whole business to be of his imagination.

Little did they guess that the fox, despite all the racket that Spider made for most of the day, had come again at the boy's lunchtime. Each time it came a little nearer to where he sat, until, on his final day of crowstarving on that particular field, it sat before him.

Slowly Spider stretched out his arm, and, gently, the fox took the food from his hand.

CHAPTER TEN

AFTER THAT FIRST so exciting ride up to Maggs'
Corner on Percy Pound's Matchless, Spider made
his own way to the field each day. He had, it
seemed, a good sense of direction and an eye for
landmarks, so that both his father and the foreman
became confident, first that he could find his way to
and from his place of work and second that having
arrived there, he would conscientiously do what he
had been told to do without any sort of supervision.
He did not own a watch, for he could not tell the
time anyway, but he seemed to know exactly when,
toward dusk, the croaks would stop work for the
day. Then so would he, plodding homeward with
that strange gait of his.

"I never seed nobody walk like that afore," Billy
Butt said to his nephews, "never in all my born
days, which, as you boys do know, are great in number. That Spider, he do put each foot down just as
if he was squashing bleddy snails. They won't need

to put the ring roller over Maggs' Corner come spring, the boy'll have firmed it up lovely with they girt boots of his. And talk about turning his toes out, he walks like a bleddy duck."

"You don't want to let Kathie Sparrow catch you talking like that, Uncle Billy," said Frank.

"I speaks as I finds," said Billy. "Allus has done, even when I were a nipper in school, don't care who 'tis. I says what I thinks to 'em, old or young, rich or poor, high or low, man or woman. 'Twould be all the same if I'd met the Queen herself, which I never did."

"Queen Mary, d'you mean?" asked Phil. "Or Queen Elizabeth?"

"Queen Victoria, of course, you girt hummock," said Billy. "I shoulda spoke my mind to she or to any of they nobs, Lady High Horse or the Duchess of Muck. The good Lord gave me a tongue and I do use it."

"You do, Uncle," said Frank and Phil. "You do."

Now Percy set the crowstarver to work on another piece of winter wheat, sown later because of a short spell of wet weather, on a very large field called Slimer's (though no one knew who Mr. Slimer had been), which lay next to Maggs' Corner, on the other side of the little spinney.

Outoverdown Farm was a rough square in shape, a thousand acres in extent, and bisected by the drove,

which ran north to south. At its northern end it was
bounded by the river Wylye, which gave the valley
its name, and by the road that ran beside it.

Nearest to river and road were the water meadows and, beyond them, a belt of goodish land
whereon the arable crops were sown. Then, to one
moving southward, the ground climbed sharply up
some rough steeps across which ran lynchets—
grassy ridges or terraces that remained from some
ancient method of cultivation—until finally, at the
top, there was the great sweep of downland that
made up the bulk of the farm.

Between the two wars these downs, thin-soiled
above the chalk, never felt the bite of the plow-
share, but soon Mister and others like him would
rip up the springy turf to grow wheat and barley
and oats in this time of trouble, enough to provide
employment for a regiment of crowstarvers.

But now the solitary one found that life on
Slimer's was a good deal less pleasant than it had
been at Maggs' Corner, for the simple reason that
the weather turned even colder—and wet to boot.
The first evening Spider came home soaked
through, bowed down by the weight of his sodden
overcoat, and Kathie was up in arms.

"If it's weather like this tomorrow," she said to
Tom, "then he's not going out and you can tell

Percy I said so, don't care if the birds eat every bit of corn. He gets tired enough as 'tis when the weather's good. He'll catch his death, standing about with nowhere to shelter. What good is it to him earning a few bob a week if we have to use it to pay for his funeral, tell me that!"

"All right, all right," said Tom. "I'll fix something up for him." And the next morning he appeared in the stables early and had a word with the foreman before the other men arrived.

So it was that, a little later, Ephraim put Em'ly to the Scotch cart and loaded onto it an old tarpaulin, some hurdles, some stakes, a coil of wire, wire cutters, a sledgehammer and crowbar, an old wooden crate, and Spider.

They went up the drove and picked up Tom and Molly at the shepherd's hut, and so on to Slimer's. Here the two men set to work to build, just inside the spinney, a rough shelter, making post holes, driving in the stakes, wiring together hurdles to make a kind of hut, before finally fixing the tarpaulin over roof and sides, allowing a flap of it to hang down over the open end to act as a door. Lastly, Tom pulled aside the flap and put the wooden crate within, upside down.

"There you are, Spider my son," he said. "Now if it comes on to rain hard, or you get a bit cold, you get in here."

"You can sit on the box and eat your bit of lunch in there, Spider," said Ephraim.

Spider looked from one to the other, and then at the new construction. "Spider's house?" he said.

"That's right," said Tom. "Show us what you're going to do, then, if it's raining."

Grinning, Spider ducked under the low opening at the front of the shelter and sat down on the crate. Then, as they knew he would, he made his usual approving comment.

"That's all right, then," said Tom. "Now then, you can give us a hand with this stuff." And together they loaded onto the Scotch cart the leftover hurdles and stakes and wire and the tools.

"Now then, sojer," said Tom. "Off you go and bang your drum and frighten them croaks." And the two men watched as Spider stumped off down the field, banging and shouting. He did not look back to see if they were watching, as an ordinary boy might have done, for he was already intent upon his job. What's more, they heard, he had enlarged his repertoire of sounds.

No longer was it just "Geddoff, croaks! Bad uns!" He also made strange noises designed to strike fear into a croak's breast—a donkey-like "Ee-orr!", a high wailing "Oo-ah! Oo-ah!" like a siren, and lastly, a bark.

"Listen to that!" said the horseman. "Anyone didn't know would swear that were a dog."

"Ar, but not *any* dog, Eph," said Tom. "That's Molly's bark." And indeed, as Molly sat listening, she shivered and whined a little at the mystery of hearing her own voice.

"It's all right, Moll," said Tom. "Jump up now." And they got up on the cart, and Ephraim laid the reins across Em'ly's back.

"He don't mind, then," he said, "being stuck up here all by himself?"

"No," said Tom. "He's happy as a pig in muck. Keeps on about a fox as comes to see him."

"Is that right?"

"Yes. He feeds it, he says. Job to believe that, though, really."

"I don't know," said Ephraim. "He's got a gift with animals. I told you, didn't I, how he was with my horses? He trusted them, they trusted him."

On the way back to the shepherd's hut they could hear the crowstarver, but then he stopped for a while, and they caught a distant, very different sound. It came from the far side of the river Wylye, but the north wind brought it clearly to their ears.

"Talk of foxes," said Tom.

It was the music of hounds.

At the sound Em'ly pricked her ears and danced

a little in an elderly, stiff-jointed way.

"Come up, you silly old mare," said Ephraim, tugging at the reins. "'Tis a main few year since you went hunting."

He pulled her to a halt and they listened. From the downlands on the opposite side of the valley the wind carried the sound clearly, the unmistakable sound of a pack of hounds in full cry on a hot scent.

"Mister'll be out, then," said Tom.

"Oh ar," said Ephraim. "They'm hunting over someone else's land, see." For though Major Yorke loved above all to ride to hounds, he was not keen to invite the local hunt to Outoverdown Farm, because of his sheep and, now, the new-sown corn.

Then Em'ly stopped her fidgeting as the distant noise ceased abruptly, and Ephraim clicked his tongue at her and they moved on.

On Slimer's, Spider, too, quiet for a moment after putting the croaks to flight, heard the noise start and then stop but thought little about it.

At midday he went into his new house and sat on the box and took his food from his pocket. But he did not eat it straightaway, waiting for his friend to come and claim a share as usual. But no one came. He could not possibly know that the cry of the pack had ceased so suddenly because the hounds had overrun and killed their fox—Spider's fox.

CHAPTER ELEVEN

ONCE THE WHEAT on Slimer's was too well established for further worry about bird damage, Spider's days as a crowstarver were, for the time being, over.

"The boy did very well, sir," Percy Pound told Mister. "D'you want me to see if I can find him some other work that he could manage?"

"By all means, Percy," Mister said. "There won't be any crowstarving for him before spring, but anytime you can give him something to do, well, I'll pay the lad on a piecework basis. Have you any idea what he does with his weekly ten shillings?"

"He gives it all to Kathie," said Percy, "and she buys him his favorite sweets out of it, licorice allsorts, never anything else."

Percy talked it over with Tom and they agreed that it would be a good idea to let the boy try his hand at a number of different jobs, to see where he could be most useful.

The first week after Spider came off Slimer's,

Percy put him with his father. But Tom soon found that there was not a lot that Spider could do to help him at that time of year, comparatively slack from a shepherd's viewpoint. Moreover, Tom, in making the rounds of his sheep, had to accommodate his long stride to the boy's plod, or else Spider would become breathless. He noted, though, that whereas the flock would bunch or run before him or the dog, they seemed to treat Spider as an honorary sheep and would stand quiet and allow him to walk in among them and even to stroke individual animals.

"He might be some use to me come lambing," Tom said to Percy, "but not right now."

"I'll give him a week up with Stan," said the foreman.

"I don't think he'll be strong enough to help shift the fold units," said Tom.

"Well, he can help collect the eggs," said Percy.

So Spider rode up with Stan Ogle in his little rubber-tired tub cart, loaded with chicken feed and pulled by Pony. But he was indeed not strong enough to help in moving the heavy folds to fresh ground each morning, and only got in the way of Red and Rhode as they helped their father. The Ogle boys were not particularly kindhearted, and they made sly jokes about Spider, which he did not understand, and laughed at him.

Stan Ogle did, on Percy's instructions, allow Spider to give a hand in collecting the eggs from his huge flock of hens, but not before he'd given the boy a stern warning about possible breakages. This meant that Spider picked up each egg with such painful care that it took him an age to clear one nest box, and then, to top it off, he tripped, carrying a full tray of eggs, and smashed all of them.

"Send un somewheres else, Percy, for the Lord's sake," said the poultryman after a few days.

So the next morning, after the rest had left the stables, the foreman said to Spider, "How'd you like to stay in here today? You like the horses, don't you?"

Spider nodded. "Good uns," he said softly.

"Well, you bide here along of Ephraim and he'll find you summat to do."

The horseman gave Spider a long-handled four-tined fork—four-grain prong, a Wiltshireman would call it—and told him to muck out Pony's empty stall, but he could soon see that while the boy was not able to handle the implement properly, he was perfectly capable of doing himself an injury. Because of his clumsy way of getting about and the enthusiasm with which he drove his fork into the straw, Ephraim could see it was only a matter of time before he would spear himself through the foot.

"Leave that for now, Spider," he said, and he took him down to the far end of the long, cobbled stables.

Here, hung upon pegs in the wall, was all the tack for the workhorses—the big straw-stuffed head collars, the slim brass hames that fitted around those collars, the reins, the blinkered headpieces, the heavy ridged saddles, the breechings, the girths. There were in all eight sets, of varying sizes, for Flower the Shire mare, for the two retired heavyweight hunters Em'ly and Jack, for the four hairy-heeled cart horses of doubtful breeding—halfway horses, Ephraim called them—and for the pony, Pony.

All this saddlery had to be kept clean and in good working order, Ephraim knew only too well, for it was he who had to do it all, apart from some occasional help from his son, Albie, and now that was no longer forthcoming.

All the brasswork—the hames, all the rings and buckles of the harnesses, the metal plates set in the saddles—had to be polished. All the leather parts of the saddlery had to be kept supple with saddle soap and wax polish. Ephraim took down a pair of hames, slender and curved, with a little brass ball on the tip of each, and from a shelf he took a tin of Brasso and some cloths. He sat down on a bench and beckoned Spider to sit beside him.

"Now watch me," he said, and he shook some Brasso onto a cloth and began to rub it into a short length of the metal with little circular motions. Then he took a clean cloth and buffed the metal till it shone. "Reckon you could do that, Spider?" he asked.

Spider nodded eagerly.

"You got to keep on doing that, all over thisyer hames, till the pair of 'em is shining bright. Take your time. I'll be down the other end mucking out, if you wants me."

Spider did indeed take his time. He was painfully slow, partly because of his innate clumsiness, partly because he was obviously determined to do the job well. And he did.

At the end of the week, the horseman took Percy Pound to show him the shining brasswork and well-polished leather of one of the eight sets of saddlery. "Guess who done that, Percy," he said.

The foreman looked at Spider. "Did you do that?" he said.

Spider gave his lopsided grin, nodding his head a great many times and hopping from foot to foot.

"Good boy!" said Percy, and he put his hand in his pocket and pulled out a sixpence.

"Here," he said. "Get yourself a few extra all-sorts."

"Took him two days to do that one set," said Ephraim, "but he kept on steady."

"I'll leave him with you for the time being, then, Eph," said Percy.

"Even at this rate, he'll have done all my tack in a couple of weeks," said the horseman. "That'll be a real help to me. 'Twas never my favorite job."

"Don't drive him too hard, mind," said Percy. "He's only a kid, after all. Give him the afternoon off, now and again."

So one day the following week Ephraim said to Spider at midday, "Well done, boy. Now then, you can have the rest of the day off."

Seeing that Spider did not understand, the horseman took him by the shoulders, propelled him toward the stable door, and said, "Off you go, there's a good lad. Have a little holiday."

"Where go?" Spider said.

"Why, to your house, of course," said Ephraim, meaning to Tom's cottage.

"Spider's house?"

"That's right."

So Spider set off. He did not know why he was going, but he knew where he had to go, so up the drove he went and off across the fields to the spinney that lay between Maggs' Corner and Slimer's, and so to his house, as he'd been told.

He pulled aside the flap and went and sat on the box and got out his lunch and began happily eating. For a moment he thought about his fox, but did not worry at not seeing it, especially as a robin now appeared on the ground in front of the shelter. Spider particularly liked robins, and he threw out some crumbs.

"Tic-tic-tic-tic," he called softly. "Tssip! Tseee!" And the robin, intrigued at hearing its own voice, hopped nearer. Soon a large number of other small birds appeared on the ground outside Spider's house—sparrows, chaffinches, hedge sparrows, titmice, and what he always called a "birdblack"— and between them they consumed a large part of Spider's lunch. All of them showed no sign of fear of the boy, but all of them disappeared in a hurry when a carrion crow dropped down.

Perhaps because it was alone, perhaps because it was not stealing corn and only croaks that did that were bad, Spider did not think of trying to frighten it away. Instead, he spoke to it in its own tongue.

"Kraa!" said Spider, realistically hoarsely, for his own voice was beginning to break, and "Kraa!" the crow replied.

Spider threw it his last crust, and it took it in its strong bill and flew up into the trees above.

Spider was very hungry that evening.

"I don't reckon I'm giving you enough for your lunch," said Kathie. "Growing boy like you."

"Birds!" said Spider with his mouth full, and then he swallowed and illustrated his meaning by giving some bird calls, the robin's, the "cheep" of sparrows and the "tseep, tseep" of the hedge sparrow, and the unmistakable song of the cock chaffinch, a cascade of a dozen notes ending in a loud "choo-ee-o!" At the same time, he mimed the throwing of bits of food.

"Giving half his lunch to the birds!" said Kathie to Tom. "I might have known."

Tom went down to the pub that evening (it had always pleased him that his local tavern should be called The Lamb) for a glass or two of the rough cider that most of the farm men drank, and there, by chance, met Ephraim Stanhope.

"Evening, Eph," he said. "Do us a favor, will you?"

"What's that?" asked the horseman.

"Let our Spider have a pocketful of tail corn to feed his blessed birds with. He give them half his lunch today. Dunno if you saw him feeding them?"

"I never," said Ephraim. "I sent him home midday."

"That's funny. Kathie never said."

"I give him the afternoon off. 'Have a little holiday,' I said. 'Go on back to your house.'"

Spider's house, thought Tom, so *that's* where he went!

He said nothing of this to Kathie, but the next day, as he and Spider set out together from the cottage, he said, "You had the afternoon off yesterday, did you?"

Spider nodded, grinning.

"Hol-i-day!" he said.

"Where'd you go, then?"

"Spider's house! Good un!"

They parted, Spider toward the stables, Tom up the drove, dog at heel. "He's happy, Moll," said Tom. "That's the main thing. Don't matter he's got no learning, don't matter he can't run and play games like other kids his age. Just so long as he's happy. Which he seems to be, whether 'tis cleaning harnesses or thinking he's a sojer, marching up and down banging his drum to frighten they croaks. Thank God he'll never be able to be a real sojer, no matter how long this war do last."

CHAPTER TWELVE

THUS FAR, THE war, although now a few months old, had not really impinged upon most people in Britain. Life in the Wylye Valley went on much as usual, and at the beginning of March 1940, Spider Sparrow once more took up his duties as crow-starver.

Percy had found work for him where he could throughout the winter, and now, with the sowing of both spring wheat and barley, there was once more need for his shouting and whistling and barking and banging, in his war against the croaks.

The spring corn was drilled on the lower grounds, not far from the lambing field, which meant that, though no longer able to use the shelter in the spinney, Spider could if need be take refuge in the shepherd's hut.

On pouring wet days (and there were many) he stayed in the lambing pens and helped his father, and at midday and in the evening they ate together, in the hut, the food that Kathie brought out for the two of them. At suppertime she waited till Spider had finished his meal and then took him back home with her.

"You've got to get your proper sleep," she said. "Your father has to do the best he can, this time of year, but you need yours, you're growing so fast."

And indeed Spider was shooting up, "like a runner bean," Tom said. He did not put on much weight but only height, it seemed, and by his fourteenth birthday he was taller than his mother and not far short of his father.

For a birthday present they gave him two things, one because it would be useful, one because they knew, from little things he had said, he very much wanted it.

The first was a big silver whistle that could hang around his neck on a lanyard.

"You blow that when you need to rest your voice," they said. "That'll put the wind up the croaks." And it did for a while, until, of course, the birds grew used to it, as indeed they'd grown used to all of Spider's noises. They flew up, and over to the next nearest piece of corn, and down again.

The other present was a knife. All the farm men carried pocketknives, and Tom had a big one with a single curved blade that he used for paring the

sheep's hooves, and for years now Spider had mur-
mured "Good un" whenever he set eyes on it. So
they bought him a really good knife with two long
blades that folded into a stout handle, metal-
capped at either end, the handle made from stag's
horn. Let in to the stag's horn was a little plate, on
which Tom had carefully scratched the initials JJS.

Kathie was not as happy about this present as
Tom. "He'll cut himself," she said.

"I've tried to teach him, but anyway, he'll
learn," said Tom.

Both were right.

A day or so after his birthday Spider, whittling
at a bit of stick with the blade of his new knife facing toward the hand in which he held the wood, cut
the ball of his thumb quite deeply, as Kathie had
said he would. But as Tom had said, he learned by
that always to cut with the blade facing away.

On his birthday something rather unusual
happened, as though in honor of the event.

They had just eaten their lunch in the hut, and
Tom told Spider not to go back to his crowstarving
but to stay a little while and help with what Tom
suspected would be a difficult birth.

One way of denoting the age of a ewe was to describe her, when young, as a two-tooth, then as a
four-tooth, and later as full-mouthed.

This ewe was a big old full-mouthed Border Leicester, and Tom had already felt around and knew that she was carrying twins. He could feel forelegs and hind legs muddled together, and now, putting a hand inside her, he began to maneuver the lambs, pushing one back, easing one forward, then turning it around till its forelegs were presented, and then, gently, drawing it.

"That's one of them," he said to Spider after he had cleared its mouth of mucus. "Here, take thisyer towel and give un a good rub."

Then he knelt down again in the straw of the pen and began work on the other. This, too, was a breech presentation—the backside trying to come out first—and again the shepherd had to push the second lamb back in order to grasp its legs, hind legs this time. Things did not seem to be going easily, and the ewe bleated loudly in pain, and Spider left the now-dry firstborn and began to stroke the mother's head. He made reassuring sheep noises, as though he were the ewe and she the lamb, and it seemed to comfort her.

Tom, meanwhile, was frowning in puzzlement, and then suddenly he began to smile as the truth dawned on him.

"Must be to celebrate your birthday, son," he said as he drew the second lamb and handed it to

Spider. Then, quite easily now, for it was released from the traffic jam of its siblings, he delivered a third lamb and placed it by the ewe's head.

"Triplets!" he said to Spider. "Wass think of that, then?"

Spider looked at the three lambs, his face splitting in a great grin. He held up a hand and counted upon the fingers. "One! Two! Three!" he said.

"That's right."

While Tom was seeing to the triplets, Spider stood stock-still, staring fixedly at their mother. After a while, he pointed to her back end and called, "Dada!"

"Yes," said Tom, "what is it?"

"Four?" said Spider, and looked quite disappointed when Tom shook his head.

Lambing over, and the spring corn no longer in need of Spider's protection, life on Outoverdown Farm followed its usual tranquil pattern, but in April things began to boil up abroad.

Poland had surrendered to the Germans not long after the outbreak of war, and in March the Russians had overrun Finland. Now Germany invaded first Denmark and Norway, in April, and then, the following month, Belgium and the Netherlands.

Between May 29 and June 4, about 338,000 Allied troops were rescued from Dunkirk.

On June 10, Percy Pound and his wife received a telegram from the War Office, regretting to inform them that their only son, Private Henry Pound of the Wiltshire Regiment, had been killed in action during the retreat.

So, for the first time, the war impinged upon the life of the village and of the farm in particular. Major and Mrs. Yorke, whose only son was training as a fighter pilot, came to the foreman's house to offer their sympathy, and in the stables all the men, including on this occasion Tom and Stan Ogle, mumbled condolences in one way or another. Only Spider said nothing, and the men knew it was because he had not understood.

Percy, though his heart was breaking and his knee hurting him abominably, received the halting words with a nod and a quiet "Thank you," and all went about their business.

And the business of the farm went on as usual, though now all (except Spider) realized that Britain was in imminent danger of invasion by the German forces.

Haymaking came and went, with every available hand helping, including Mister driving the old Lea-Francis with a sweep on the front of it, and soon it was September and harvesttime.

In the hayfield Spider had not been allowed to

use a fork but had been given a wooden rake, to pull in the outermost swath from the headlands and to tidy up odd corners. All this he did very meticulously but very, very slowly.

At harvesttime he carried sheaves of wheat or of barley to the other men, who set them up in stooks. The binder on its journey around the field would throw out the tied sheaves, which must then be collected and arranged in stooks of six or eight, each sheaf leaning against one opposite, butts to ground, heads upward forming a kind of tent or tunnel, for maximum drying on the one hand and, should the weather break, for maximum protection.

For Spider, a stook was another kind of house, and he liked to creep into one to eat his lunch. Until, of course, he knocked one down and was sworn at. But mostly the men treated him kindly. He was also useful for running errands (though running was a misnomer), and one day, a beautiful September day, Percy sent him back down to the farm to fetch something.

They were harvesting barley at the southernmost end of the farm, where Mister had a piece of virgin downland plowed up, and all the men were at work pitching the now-dry sheaves up onto the wagons. The biggest of all was drawn by Flower, with Jack in the traces in front of her. Two other wagons were drawn by two of the hairy heels, and Em'ly pulled the Scotch cart.

Deftly the pitchers speared each sheaf on their two-grain prongs and then threw them up onto the wagons, and deftly the loaders on top built their loads, butts facing outward, building quickly, carefully, skillfully, so that the whole would be secure on its bumpy journey to the stack.

It was a traditional English country scene, as peaceful as could be. But suddenly the war intruded.

The first the men heard was a distant roar of engines, and then as they leaned upon their pitchforks and looked about, they saw, approaching at top speed, two fighter aircraft. The sun was in the men's eyes, and they could not see that the leading plane had black crosses on its wings, but then suddenly they heard the rattle of machine-gun fire from the chasing aircraft. Then the two planes were directly above them, and they could see RAF roundels on the curved wings of the pursuing Spitfire. The German plane—a Messerschmitt—rocked in the hail of fire pouring into it and its engine began to stutter. It dropped lower and lower, over Tom's sheep a quarter of a mile away, which ran in a panic-stricken white blanket, and over a bunch of the Irish heifers half a mile away, which galloped and buckjumped wildly in all directions, and then at last, losing height all the while, disappeared from sight over the shoulder of the downs. The watching men, all but one of whom had never in their lives heard a shot fired in anger, were cheering wildly at the outcome of this single combat. But Percy Pound, whose knee the Germans had smashed and whose son the Germans had killed, stood silent. He tried to make himself hope that the pilot would survive, but failed.

Meanwhile, Spider, marching down the drove on his errand, suddenly heard the noise of the aircraft and then the rattle of the firing, and he stopped and stood in a gateway, staring back up. He saw one airplane high above, twisting itself in what, though he did not know it, was a victory roll, and then he saw, coming over the shoulder of the hill, another. It was quite silent, this second plane, for its engine was dead, and as the Luftwaffe pilot looked desperately for somewhere safe to land, it dropped lower and lower, the wind whistling past its rocking wings. Spider stood rooted to the ground as the Messerschmitt swept directly toward him.

CHAPTER THIRTEEN

THE ENORMOUS WIND of the fighter passing only a few yards above his head knocked Spider flat, and when he picked himself up, it was to see the plane, its landing gear damaged and useless, sliding fast on its belly across the grass of the field that led toward Slimer's.

At the end of the field it ran into a four-strand barbed-wire fence, which snapped like a string but nevertheless acted as a brake on its further progress, and it slid around and came to a shuddering halt.

Spider, watching, saw a figure climb out of the cockpit and jump to the ground. The German pilot, miraculously unhurt, was standing uncertainly beside his aircraft when he heard, coming from the higher ground above, the noise of a farm tractor.

As with any hunted animal, his immediate thought was to try to evade capture, to find somewhere to hide from possible pursuers, and he ran off across the stubble, clumsily in his flying suit and boots, making for the nearest cover. He did not look behind him as he ran, but had he done so, he would have seen the figure of a tall, thin boy, hurrying, splayfooted, toward the crashed plane.

When his aircraft had disappeared from the sight of the men in the harvest field, the general impulse was to rush off in the direction it had taken. The brothers Red and Rhode Ogle, the most impulsive, were in the act of doing so when Percy called them back.

"Steady, you two," he said. "You wait a minute." Don't want them all getting there before me, he thought, which they would do, even old Billy, with this gammy leg of mine. I've got most reason to be keen to see a dead German.

In addition to the horse-drawn wagons, they were using the Fordson tractor and its trailer, which chanced at that time to be empty, so Percy told Ephraim and Stan Ogle to stay with the horses, and he and the rest climbed onto the trailer. Frank started up the tractor, and away they went toward the top of the drove: Percy and Tom and Red and Rhode and Phil and Billy Butt.

"Wonder where he come down?" said Tom to Percy. "Nowhere near Spider, I hope. It'd scare the lad to death."

Billy was in a bloodthirsty mood. He alone had brought his pitchfork with him, and, as they bounced about on the trailer, Frank driving at top speed down the bumpy drove, he told everyone, in his loud, shrill voice, just what he would do with it.

"If so be the bagger's alive," he squeaked, "old Billy'll soon put that right. Stick un right through his bleddy German guts I shall, which I shoulda done with the bayonet if I'd been a sojer. I'd a made a bleddy good sojer, I would, thee'st know, won one of they Victorian Crosses I shouldn't be surprised, but there, I were too old when the war come."

"You coulda fought in the Boer War, though, Billy, couldn't you?" asked Rhode Ogle innocently, but before Billy could answer, they came in sight of the downed plane.

Turning off the drove, the tractor roared across the grass toward the wreckage. Beside it, they could see, a figure was standing, and Billy, whose eyesight was not what it had been, cried excitedly, "There, lookzee, the bagger's alive!" and he waved his pitchfork in the air and shouted, "Now then, you bleddy German, I'm going to stick thisyer pick in thy bleddy arse!"

"Bide quiet, Billy," said Tom as they neared the plane. "That's no German, that's our Spider."

"Where be the pilot, then?" asked Phil Butt.

"Dead in the cockpit, maybe," said Percy. I hope, he thought savagely.

But the cockpit was empty, they found as they inspected the Messerschmitt and saw the bullet holes and tears in fuselage and wings, the twisted and bent propeller.

"Where is he, then, Spider?" squeaked Billy, still bursting with bloodlust. "Didst see un? Dost know where he's gone to? He can't be far. Where's he to?"

"Steady, Billy," said Percy. "Let Tom ask him."

"Did you see the man, Spider?" said Tom.

Spider nodded.

"Where'd he go?"

Spider pointed toward Slimer's.

"He's in the spinney," said Tom.

"Come on!" cried Billy.

"Wait," said Percy. "He may be armed. It's no good rushing in there, mad-headed. Frank, you drive the tractor 'round the back, by Maggs' Corner, in case he breaks that way. Phil, you and Billy stay on the trailer and go with him, and you two Ogle boys, and then spread yourselves 'round the back of the spinney. We'll go in the front. If you see him and he comes out with his hands up, all well and good, but if he's got a pistol, don't try anything till we get help. And you, Billy, give me that pitchfork of yourn."

Once he was satisfied that his men had surrounded the spinney, Percy shouted, "Come on out
with your hands up!" and then, remembering the
phrase from that other war, "*Hände hoch!*" At this,
some wood pigeons crashed out of the ash trees,
but there was no sign of the fugitive.

Spider pulled at Tom's arm.

"What is it?" the shepherd said.

"Spider's house," said the boy.

"Like as not," said Tom to Percy.

"Come on, then," said the foreman. "You keep
behind me and keep the boy behind you." And he
limped forward into the edge of the spinney, pitchfork held before him.

Spider's house was partly overgrown now.
Climbing plants had crept up its sides, and it was
surrounded by a bed of stinging nettles. A pathway
through the nettles had been freshly crushed, they
could see.

"He's in there," said Percy softly. "Tom, you
pull the flap of the tarpaulin back." And he stood
opposite the entry to the shelter, pitchfork at the
ready, his weight forward on his good leg.

"Keep behind me, Spider," said Tom, and he
pulled back the flap.

"Right," said Percy. "Come on out, you devil."

Then, bending under the low entry, there

emerged from Spider's house a slim, boyish figure, with fair curly hair and blue eyes.

"*Kamerad,*" said the German pilot quietly as he raised his hands above his head. He managed a nervous smile.

Percy Pound stared into those blue eyes, and all of a sudden, as he did so, he experienced a dramatic change of mood. He found himself forgetting his anger and his hatred for any member of this nation that had killed his son, and instead he felt a stab of pity and an enormous sorrow for the madness of mankind.

He lowered the pitchfork.

Oh, dear God, he thought, he looks so much like our Henry.

CHAPTER FOURTEEN

THE WAR IN the air played quite a part in the life of Outoverdown Farm that September, as the Battle of Britain was fought. Hardly had the wrecked Messerschmitt been removed than another official telegram arrived, this time for Major and Mrs. Yorke. Mercifully, it was news not of death, but of capture.

Their only son, Pilot Officer Hugh Yorke, had been shot down over the French coast. In a kind of mirror image of the incident on the farm, he had managed to land his stricken Hurricane and had been taken prisoner.

"First Percy's boy, now Mister's boy," said Tom to Kathie. "These things often come in threes. Will it be Albie Stanhope next, d'you think?"

"He was home on leave not long ago, wasn't he?" said Kathie.

"Yes, he's stationed up in the north of the county, I think, not all that far away," said Tom.

*   *   *

"How's your Albie, then?" said the shepherd to the horseman when they next met.

"Oh, he's fallen on his feet, he has," said Ephraim. "They've gone mechanized, his lot have, thee'st know, riding on Bren carriers instead of horses, but our Albie's C.O., he's a hunting man, like Mister, and he keeps a couple of horses and gets a day out now and again, and what d'you think?"

"I bet I know," said Tom. "Albie's got the job of looking after them."

Ephraim nodded.

"Rides 'em out, what's more."

"Cushy young devil," said Tom. "Wass think about Mister's boy, then?"

"He's alive, anyway," said Ephraim. Unlike Percy's son, each man thought.

"One thing," said the horseman. "Your lad's safe, whatever happens."

Tom, of course, had no means of knowing how close Spider had been to death in the path of the stricken plane, and Spider had no means of telling him.

Afterward, he had spread his arms wide and run clumsily toward Tom, making swooshing noises, but he had not the powers of speech to describe what happened.

On any farm at any time there are of course hazards that a boy might have to face, but in general Spider was kept well away from machinery. As to danger from livestock, no one worried overly, because of the boy's strange empathy with all living creatures.

Only recently he had been out with Tom when they passed near a bunch of the Irish heifers with their bull. Percy Pound had come roaring up the drove on his motorbike and had stopped to talk to the shepherd. Looking around after Percy had gone, Tom saw that Spider had walked in among the cattle and was making directly for the Aberdeen Angus bull. Hornless and placid-natured the animal might be, but that great heavy head could do a great deal of damage if swung at the boy in anger or irritation.

But no, before Tom could say or do anything, Spider reached the bull and began to pat and stroke it, while the big black animal stood stock-still, apparently enjoying this attention. To top it off, Spider took hold of the brass ring in the bull's nose and led it over to his father and halted before him.

"He's a good un, Dada," he said.

"Never seen anything like it," said Tom to Percy later. "I said to him, 'Come on now, Spider, bulls is dangerous, you know,' so he lets go of the ring and comes on along of me. But then as we went on across the field, there's the old bull walking along a couple of paces behind us, just like a big dog following his master, wanting a pat."

But the danger into which Spider was shortly to fall was one that Tom and Kathie had never considered. The river Wylye was a gently flowing chalk stream that meandered its way through the meadows, spanned here and there by pretty stone bridges that carried the road back and forth across it. The waters of the stream were clear, bedded with gravel and festooned with waving weed, and in them were trout and perch and roach and rudd and the occasional predatory pike.

The Wylye formed one boundary, the northern, of Outoverdown Farm, and near the village there were a couple of pools where some of the children swam on hot summer days. Spider did not, of course. Neither Tom nor Kathie could swim, so the idea of teaching Spider to do so never occurred to them. There was no reason for him to go into the water.

But Spider in his free time often walked by the river. He liked to look at the wild birds there—the swans and the ducks, the moorhens and dabchicks, the brilliant flashing kingfishers—all of which accepted his quiet presence without worry. He liked to watch the water voles swimming across, and one day he was fortunate enough to set eyes upon a creature he'd never seen before: a sleek brown animal with a round, cat-like head and a long, ruddery tail. He was leaning on the parapet of a bridge when he saw it, twisting and twirling beneath the clear water as it chased a fish.

He found its picture in his book that evening and showed it to his parents.

"What that?" he said.

"That's an otter," they said. "Did you see one?"

Spider nodded rapidly, excitedly. He spent a long time staring at the picture and tracing the outline of the creature with a finger and mouthing to himself. Passing close to him, Kathie heard him saying, "Hotter. Good un. Hotter. Good un. Good Hotter."

For Percy Pound the foreman, the river Wylye held a special magic. He had been born by it, in a village some miles farther downstream, and, apart from those grim years of fighting in France, had lived near it all his life.

Percy was not a churchgoing man. The peace of God passed his understanding (though he had called upon His name often enough in the trenches), but every Sunday morning he would leave his house and walk past the farmyard and then down a grassy lane till he reached the banks of the Wylye. Here, standing beside its rippling tranquility, looking into its clear depths, and listening to its gentle song, he drew strength and solace. Without ever setting foot in the river, he felt nonetheless that he could immerse himself in it and wash away all stress and worry.

As a younger man, he came alone on these Sunday pilgrimages, but then, once his son, Henry, was old enough, they would go together. Now he was always alone again by the riverside, and at the end of one week he stood at a favorite spot, gazing down a favorite reach toward a stone bridge beneath whose arch the Wylye softly ran and on whose parapet he and his son had so often leaned and looked down at the trout lying in the clear water, heads pointing upstream, each fish's fins and tail working gently to hold its place against the gentle current.

Now, as Percy looked, he saw that there was a figure that appeared to be sitting upon the parapet of the bridge, and he felt an actual pain in his heart at the knowledge that it was not Henry, that it could never again be Henry.

Spider had walked to the bridge that Sunday in hopes that he might there see again the "hotter." For a while he leaned upon the low stone wall, looking down into the water and seeing fish but no mammal. A moorhen swam out of the bankside reeds, and Spider called to it in its own voice— "Prrruk!" and "Kik! Kik! Kik!"—and it answered. Then he took from his pocket his knife with the stag's horn handle and began to whittle at a stick he was carrying, remembering to cut away from himself. For comfort, he swung his legs (clumsily, of course) over the wall and sat upon it, legs dangling above the water. There was a knot in the piece of wood that resisted the knife blade, and as he cut harder at it, the blade suddenly sliced through the obstruction and Spider almost lost his balance.

Striving to regain it, he dropped the knife. It hit the water with a small splash and sank, the silver of its blade flashing, fish-like, as it fell to the riverbed, here some six feet deep, and settled upon the graveled bottom.

Spider, leaning far out over the parapet in anguish at the loss of his treasure, then lost his balance completely and fell, all anyhow, into the river.

Percy, watching, saw the sudden fall from the bridge of the unknown figure, and then heard a loud yell, a yell of fear, a yell that would have frightened any croak and was coming, the foreman recognized, from the throat of the crowstarver himself.

As Percy hurried along the bank as fast as his

crippled knee would allow, he heard the noise stop and saw the struggling figure submerge and then surface again and let out a further strangled shout. Percy was no swimmer, but by some mercy (the mercy perhaps of Him, whom at that very moment other villagers were worshiping) he was carrying the long blackthorn thumbstick he always took on his Sunday walk, and now he managed to wade in far enough to hold out the stick for the boy to grasp.

"Hold on, Spider, hold on tight!" gasped the breathless foreman, and Spider, whose last breath could not have been far off, somehow found strength to obey.

Had the current been strong, things might have gone badly, but the Wylye, as it mostly did, flowed slowly, and Percy managed to grab the boy by his coat collar and drag him to the bank. Spider promptly threw up a great deal of water and then lay gasping, his breathing fast and shallow, his eyes wide in remembered terror.

"Oh, Percy, you saved his life!" cried Kathie later. "Oh, how grateful we are to you!"

"We are," said Tom. "I hope Spider was. He thanked you, did he?"

"Well, not at first," said Percy. "Once he got his

voice and his breath back, all he could say was 'knife.' I didn't know what he was on about, but then after a bit he takes my hand and pulls me up onto the bridge and points down into the water and says, 'Knife! Knife!' He must have dropped it in."

"We'll get him another," said Tom. It's only a knife that's lost, he thought, we've still got our son. Not like poor old Percy. And then he saw the foreman smile at him tiredly, and realized that he knew what that thought was.

"It's all right, Tom," said Percy. "It's all right."

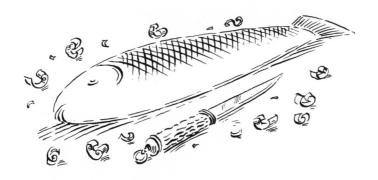

CHAPTER FIFTEEN

IN FACT, TOM did not have to buy a replacement knife for Spider. The very next day he was walking up the drove toward his hut, his new puppy at heel. He was remembering walking thus once and speaking to Molly, telling her that nothing else mattered as long as Spider was happy. He suspected then that the days of his old dog—and she was very old— were numbered, for she had bad arthritis and was in pain, and indeed shortly afterward Tom had had her put to sleep. Explaining it to Spider had been difficult, but Molly's replacement, a puppy that Tom called Moss, soon took her place in the boy's affections.

Now the shepherd heard the clop of hooves and saw his employer riding down the drove toward him.

"Morning, Tom," said Mister as he reined in Sturdiboy. "How's the new puppy doing?"

"He'll be all right, sir," Tom said. "He's got a lot to learn, but he's learning it."

"And that boy of yours?"

That boy of mine, thought Tom, is lucky to be alive today. And he told Mister the tale of yesterday's drama.

"Mr. Pound rescued him, you say?" said Major Yorke. "Good show! No harm done, then, in the end?"

"No, sir. The boy lost his precious knife, that's all, but I'll get him another one."

"Why not let me buy him one?" said Mister. "I'd like to. What was it like, this knife?"

"Matter of fact, you can see it, sir, on your way home, if you're going by the little bridge. You can see it, lying in the bottom, clear as can be, but it's in deepish water, no way of getting it out."

As well as being a hunting man, Major Yorke was a keen fisherman. Ten minutes later, crossing the bridge, he leaned out of his saddle and looked down and saw the knife. It had, he was pleased to see, a little ring at one end, a ring in which, with a lot of luck and a great deal of patience, a hook might catch. Need a biggish hook, he thought, like the one I use for pike. And he rode on home to fetch a rod.

Later that day, Kathie was giving Tom and Spider their tea when there was a knock at the cottage door, at which Moss barked. She went to open it, to find the farmer standing outside in the darkness.

"May I come in?" he said. "I have a surprise for your boy." And once inside, he took from his pocket something wrapped in a piece of rag, something that he had oiled, something at the sight of which Spider's jaw dropped.

Mister handed it to him, smiling.

"You've surely not been in the river, sir?" Tom said.

"No, no," said Mister. "I've been fishing. I dropped a line off the bridge and managed to hook it. Took a bit of patience, I don't mind telling you. Each time I nearly succeeded, the current would beat me at the last minute, so I put a little lead sinker on to weight the hook and managed to get it through the ring at last. I tell you, when I pulled it up, I was as proud as if I'd landed a good-sized trout."

"Oh, we are grateful, sir," said Kathie. "Spider, what d'you say?"

Spider stood, grinning hugely. He looked at his parents. "Spider's knife," he said. Then he looked at Mister and pointed a finger at him. "He's a good un," he said.

Before its loss, Spider had only used his knife in a fairly aimless way, whittling at odd sticks and bits of wood with no particular end in view. But after its recovery, he began to make use of it constructively, in fact to carve things with it. Unsurprisingly, he carved animals. Maybe it began because he picked up a piece of wood that in shape already resembled some creature or other, but before long he succeeded in carving what looked quite like a dog. He made several of these, improving all the while, until one day he came into the cottage kitchen, where Kathie was baking, and thrust something into her floury hand.

"For Mum," he said.

"What is it?" said Kathie.

"Moss," said Spider, and indeed Kathie could now see clearly that the carving was, apart from color, of course, a rough representation of a Border collie.

"Oh, thank you, Spider my love," said Kathie. "There's clever you are!"

Tom said much the same, some days later, when he, too, received a present.

"Barrit," said Spider, "for Dada." And a pretty good rabbit it was, too, sitting up, ears pricked, alert for danger.

Neither Kathie nor Tom knew anything about naïve art or indeed art of any kind, but they could see now that Spider, despite all his handicaps, had some gift for carving in wood. His next efforts proved this beyond doubt.

Though there was much about the world that

Spider did not understand, his recent experience had left him with two definite impressions: The foreman had pulled him out of the nasty cold river, and the farmer had rescued his most prized possession, his knife. Now that he had made presents for the two most important people in his life, his mother and father, he would make two more for the men who had helped him. The common element that bound both men to him was, in his mind, water, and now he set to work to make two more models, both of water creatures.

When the first of them was ready, he took it down to the stables with him in the pocket of the old army overcoat, which had once been much too long for him but was not now.

Percy Pound usually left Spider till last when giving out his morning orders, and so the other farm men had gone and there was no one else in the stables except for the horseman down at the far end when Spider approached the foreman and, pulling the gift from his pocket, offered it to him.

"For Per-cy," he said.

Percy took the carving. It was of a long, low, short-legged animal with a round head like a cat and a long, tapering tail. It was brown in color, for Spider had by chance made it from a piece of chestnut wood.

"For me?" said Percy.

Spider nodded. "Hotter," he said.

"I can see it is," said Percy. "A right good likeness, too. Thank you, boy, thank you. I shall treasure it."

The model Spider next made was of a fish. He had cut this from a piece of yew, so that the wood was red in color, and he had even scratched with painstaking care a pattern of scales upon it with his knife point.

"Fish," he said proudly as he showed it to his parents.

"It's lovely," they said.

"For Mis-ter," he said.

In all the years he had worked at Outoverdown Farm, Tom had never actually been to the Yorkes' house. It was not the original farmhouse, a modest building adjoining the farmyard, in which Percy Pound and his family lived, but a rather more imposing manor house just outside the village, with stabling and a fine garden.

Rather than go to it, Tom and Kathie decided that the best plan would be to intercept Mister and his wife after church. They themselves were not churchgoers, but they knew that the Yorkes were, so the next Sunday morning they all stood by the lych gate waiting, Spider carrying his gift, which Kathie had carefully wrapped. When Mister and his wife came down the church path, Tom pushed Spider forward.

"Excuse me, sir," Tom said. "My boy's got something for you."

Spider held out the wrapped fish. "For Mis-ter," he said.

The farmer smiled. In his own house his wife always referred to him as "the Major" when talking to the servants, and on the hunting field he was "Major Yorke," but he knew quite well what the farm men called him, though never to his face.

"A present?" he said.

Spider nodded.

"It's his way of thanking you," said Tom, "for getting his knife out of the river."

The farmer unwrapped the fish carving and held it out for his wife to see. "Just look at that!" he said.

"That's lovely!" Mrs. Yorke said.

"You made that, Spider?" asked Mister, and he could not keep a note of incredulity from his voice.

Spider nodded.

"He's carved quite a few things lately," Kathie said.

"With that knife you fished up for him," added Tom.

"How glad I am that I did," said Mister, and

they all smiled: the Sparrows with pride in Spider, the Yorkes with pleasure at the realization that this poor damaged boy could make such an object. Spider smiled because the rest were smiling.

Not long afterward, Spider was sitting on the bank of the Wylye, listening and watching and mimicking the cries of the waterfowl, when he suddenly saw a movement on the far bank. The river was not wide at this point, and directly opposite Spider a willow leaned out at an angle over the water. Among the exposed roots of this tree there was a sizable dark hole, and it was in this hole that he saw the movement.

Then he saw the round face of an otter looking out. The animal was looking directly at him, testing the wind with upraised head, a wind that must have carried the boy's scent. But instead of immediately disappearing back into its holt, as any other otter would have done at the sight of a human so close, it gave a short, sharp whistle and came out and down to the water's edge. Then a second, slightly smaller otter emerged from the mouth of the holt and came to join its mate, and they both slipped into the river.

Spider sat, still and silent, seeing only strings of bubbles rising to the surface as the pair hunted in partnership. Presently they both suddenly appeared and hauled themselves out, oily-smooth, on the near bank right below him.

The male had a big fish in his mouth, and after some noisy bickering, he and his mate settled down to eat it, taking not the slightest notice of the watcher on the bank above.

No one would have believed Spider if he had had the power to describe the utter fearlessness of these wild animals, almost within touching distance of him, but Kathie believed him, implicitly, when he came in that evening and told her, in his limited way, what he had seen.

"Hotter!" he said to her, and then he put a forefinger crossways between his teeth and made chewing faces. "Fish!" he said, and then in his excitement he put together what was without doubt the longest sentence he had ever spoken in his life. "Hotter!" he said again. "One, two hotters, catch big fish, eat big fish, Spider see!"

CHAPTER SIXTEEN

ABOVE ALL THINGS, Mister loved horses. As an infant, he had ridden before he could walk, and though he had always lived surrounded by dogs and had, since taking over the farm, a good deal of pride and interest in his cattle, his sheep, and his poultry, the horse was for him the most beautiful of God's creatures.

In the Great War he had been a cavalryman, commanding a squadron of the 17th/21st Lancers (and, as things turned out, he thanked God that he had not been a foot soldier).

He hated to part with a horse, and so, apart from Em'ly and Jack, now working for Ephraim Stanhope in the cart horse stables, there were several others, retired from the hunting field on account of age and loss of pace, that lived a happy retirement up on the downs. Not only did Major Yorke dislike selling such old friends, he was also a sucker for acquiring new ones, and only the fact that his wife reined him in very tightly—especially on his Irish trips—stopped Outoverdown Farm from being covered in horses.

One day, however, when Mrs. Yorke was away visiting relatives, a most intriguing advertisement caught Mister's eye. There had been an American traveling road show in the county, a kind of blend of circus and fair, one of whose attractions had been a rodeo. Now the whole outfit was packing up and returning to the States, and the owners had decided to sell all the rodeo horses—six of them—rather than ship them back home.

The broncos, as the advertisement styled them, were to be sold at auction in Salisbury Market.

At this sale, perhaps because he was temporarily free of Mrs. Yorke's restraining hand, perhaps because no one else seemed especially keen to bid for these half-dozen rather wild-looking beasts, Mister had a rush of blood to the head and bought all of them.

When the hauler arrived back at Outoverdown Farm with them, Mister was waiting, with the horseman, at the junction of the road with the drove, up which Percy Pound had already ridden his motorbike. He would open the gate into the most southerly piece of downland, and then wait there to turn the horses in, for the drove continued on beyond the boundary of the farm, until it eventually met the next main road.

"We're going to run them up into the Far Hanging. They're a bit on the frisky side, I think, so they can let some steam off for a while and then we'll see what we can do with them," said Mister.

"Too much to handle, are they, sir?" asked Ephraim as the hauler was unscrewing the clamps prior to letting down the tailgate of the cattle truck.

"I don't know about that," said Mister. "To tell you the truth, Ephraim, I bought them because I felt sorry for 'em, I suppose. They haven't had much of a life—these rodeo chaps, they put a cinch around the horse's belly and draw it up tight, to make 'em buck, you know, bloody cruel."

At this point, the hauler dropped the tailgate and opened out its wings. Then suddenly there was a violent explosion from the dark interior, and out rushed the rodeo horses, who thundered down the tailgate and set off up the drove, neighing and whinnying, leaping and kicking like mad things, as though this was their first taste of freedom for ages, which it probably was.

"They'm bucking broncos, all right, sir," said Ephraim.

He just had time to see—before they settled into a gallop—that they were strong-looking animals of unusual colors. Four were piebalds, one a pale red, one a grayish yellow, or, as the sale catalog listed them, using American terms: "Four pintos, one sorrel, one buckskin."

Farmer and horseman began the long walk up the drove after the horses, but before they had gone very far, they heard the noise of the foreman's motorbike returning.

"You got a right lot there, sir," he said grumpily as he stopped beside them (the wind was sharp and his knee was hurting). "Take some breaking, they will. They come up to me full gallop and then off and away over the Far Hanging like the wind. Wouldn't surprise me if they was to jump the boundary fence and keep going. They could be in Dorset by tonight. Mebbe they're making for America. Best place for 'em, from what I could see."

"Oh, they'll be all right," said Mister. "They'll soon settle down."

But they didn't.

Over the next few days they behaved like the wild creatures they were: mustangs, feral horses rounded up specifically to be used in a "Wild West" show. For all their captive lives they had been used to a routine wherein they were penned while some likely lad was lowered onto one or the other of them. Then the cinch would be tightened and the pen door opened, and out into the makeshift ring would go the bronco, kicking madly against the pain of the cinch, while the amateur cowboy on its back promptly fell off it.

Now they were free again, and the Wiltshire downs were a fair substitute for their native prairies, and they had no intention of ever being caught again.

Each day Mister rode out into the Far Hanging on his big bay, and each day, at the sight of him, or of Percy on his motorbike, or of Tom on foot among his ewes in a neighboring piece, the broncos would kick up their heels and gallop away into the distance.

Mister consulted the horseman, and Ephraim said that the only thing to do was to drive them into a confined space where it might be possible to handle them.

"Round 'em up and corral them, eh?" said Mister. "Like the cowboys do in the movies!"

"Don't know about that, sir," said Ephraim. "I never bin to the talkies. I only ever went once to the cinema in Warminster, to see that Charlie Chaplin. But the lambing pens'd be the only place."

Out of the lambing season, Tom Sparrow did not use the stone-walled yard in which he set up his pens, except perhaps to house the occasional sick ewe, and often the shepherd's hut, with Flower in the shafts, would be hauled out to some handier location. So now it was an easy matter to stack the hurdles of the pens to make space for the broncos within the walled enclosure. But first they must be rounded up.

Mister planned this operation with military precision, to be undertaken by cavalry, supported by infantry. All the farm staff would take part. It would be spearheaded by three mounted men, himself on Sturdiboy, and Ephraim Stanhope and his soldier son, Albie, who chanced to be home on leave, riding the two ex-hunters, Em'ly and Jack.

They would enter the Far Hanging and between them drive the broncos out through the gate that led into the drove. Above this gateway, to turn the animals down, would be stationed the poultryman and his two sons. Toward the lower end of the drove Percy Pound and Tom Sparrow and Spider and the three Butts would bar the further progress of the broncos and turn them in through the gate of the walled yard.

At first the operation looked doomed to failure. Hard as Mister and the two Stanhopes galloped, the six wild horses ran rings around them, but eventually, by good luck, the riders herded them

close enough to the open gate for them to see it—
and to see it as a place of escape. Through it they
dashed, to be greeted by a wild chorus of yells from
the three Ogles, and away they galloped down the
drove, till they met the other section of the infantry
and another loud hullabaloo that turned them into
the yard. Then the gate was slammed shut behind
them. When the horsemen and the Ogles arrived,
it was to find the broncos standing bunched and
blowing, flanks heaving, the steam rising from their
odd-colored coats.

They had circled the yard at top speed, trying
madly to find an escape route. But the stone wall
was too high, and on the top bar of the gate, over
which they might have been able to jump, Tom and
the others sat and so barred that way out.

Once the cavalry had dismounted and tethered
their horses, the scene was set for the strangest
confrontation ever to take place on Outoverdown
Farm. Inside the yard were six American-bred
broncos. Outside it, eleven men and a boy looked
on.

"Right," said Mister. "Let's get a halter on one
of them, and then we can tie him up and catch the
rest one at a time."

There was a moment's silence, all hoping that
someone else would be chosen to go in among

those snorting wild-eyed brutes, and then Billy Butt voiced the thoughts of all.

"Begging your pardon, sir," he squeaked, "but I don't want to go in with they baggers. Now, years ago, when I was a young chap, I might have risked me life and me limb in amongst they bleddy things, but I bain't so quick on me feet as I was, thee'st know, and I don't want to make our Martha a widder."

"What we need, sir, is some kind of pen to run them into," said Percy. "Otherwise someone's going to get killed."

"'Tis they baggers want killing," said Billy to his nephews while farmer and foreman were talking. "There's only one proper place for they bleddy mad-headed things and that's the knacker's yard. The dear Lord only knows what Mister were a-thinking about, buying they. Cats' meat, that's all they'm fit for."

"Save thy breath, Billy," said Ephraim. "This here's my job." And halter in hand, he advanced upon the six, who immediately erupted in a wild explosion of movement and noise, bucking and neighing. Hooves flashed everywhere as they lashed out at the horseman. Suddenly, struck by the rump of one of the broncos as it whirled around, the horseman lost his footing and fell and lay on the ground in imminent danger of being trampled.

Before anyone else could move, Spider got down from the gate on which he had been sitting beside Tom, and shambled, splayfooted, out toward the squealing, clattering horses.

Instantly they drew back from the fallen man and stood watching the boy, every head turned toward him. They trembled a little and blew, and some hooves stamped, but ears were pricked, not laid back, and teeth were not bared. All the watchers were shouting: at Spider to come back, at Ephraim, now on his feet again, to get out of harm's way, which he did.

"Keep quiet, all of you," said Tom. "Don't shout no more, don't start 'em off." And in the silence that followed his words, Mister and his men could hear the noise the boy was making. It was a soft snickering noise such as one horse makes on greeting another, and a couple of the wild horses snickered in reply.

Then Spider reached the foremost of the six, a big flashily marked pinto, and reached out a hand to its muzzle and began to stroke it, at the same time making the bubbly blowing sound that a horse makes through its nostrils.

"Good un!" said Spider softly to the horse as he stroked, and at the sound of his voice the other three pintos and the sorrel and the buckskin pushed gently forward, seemingly anxious for their share of attention.

It was left to Billy Butt to encapsulate—in a few words, for once—the feelings of all.

"Well, I'm jiggered!" he said softly. "Well, I'm bleddy well jiggered!"

CHAPTER SEVENTEEN

MISTER USED MORE moderate language when describing the event to his wife. (On her return, he'd made a clean breast of his purchases and had, he hoped, been partially forgiven.)

"Never have I seen such an astonishing thing," he said now. "Talk about Daniel walking into the lion's den. He saved Ephraim from serious injury, no doubt about it. Handicapped and backward that boy may be, but he has this extraordinary gift with animals."

"An *idiot savant*," Mrs. Yorke said, pronouncing the French phrase in a proper accent.

"Eh? What's that mean?"

"Someone who is mentally subnormal but yet displays outstanding talent in a particular area."

"Yes, right, that's it exactly," said Mister. "With young Spider's help, I'm sure we shall be able to break those animals."

"I've never liked the term 'break' when talking

of horses," his wife said. "By what you've described, the boy is not going to break but to 'gentle' these broncos—which I still think you were extremely foolish to buy."

"I was, my dear, I was."

"And if he succeeds by kindness, then I think you will owe him a great debt of gratitude."

"I certainly shall. Though it's not much good giving the boy money, and if I gave it to the Sparrows, that'd be rather missing the point, wouldn't it? What d'you suggest I should do?"

"I'll think of something," said Mrs. Yorke.

The next day Mister had a word with Percy and Percy spoke to Ephraim and Ephraim talked to Tom.

The upshot of their discussion was that the broncos should remain in the yard—lambing would not start for six weeks or so yet—and there be hand-fed. Spider would spend as much time as possible with them, in this gap between his winter and his spring crowstarving, but the horseman would be on hand, in case the boy needed help or advice. So began a quite new routine for the crowstarver.

Each morning after he had finished essential stable work, Ephraim would put Em'ly or Jack in the Scotch cart, and he and Spider would ride up

the drove to the lambing pen yard. Then the broncos would be fed and watered by Spider—for they
were still very suspicious of Ephraim—and then he
would spend some hours among them, touching,
stroking, patting, in fact, as Mrs. Yorke had said,
"gentling" them, all the while communicating with
them either in his few staccato phrases or by making comfortable horse sounds.

He always carried a rope halter, which Ephraim
had taught him how to use, and he showed this to
the broncos, letting them sniff at it, laying it against
each neck in turn, until the day came when he was
able to slip it over the head of one. It was, once
again, the biggest of the pintos, the dominant animal in the little herd, and as Spider led him around,
the others all followed, as though anxious to be
next. Within a couple of hours all the rest—the
sorrel, the buckskin, and the other three pintos—
had submitted to the halter.

Within a couple of weeks the broncos would
allow Ephraim to come among them, though at
first only if accompanied by Spider, but before too
long the horseman was permitted to lead them
about, and it was becoming plain that the six wild
horses were wild no longer, but would, in due
course, make obedient, cooperative mounts, each
happy to carry upon its back one of those humans

that now, thanks to Spider, they did not anymore fear or hate.

Then the time arrived when Spider's reward for all this was decided upon. Mrs. Yorke thought of the idea, as she'd said she would, and Major Yorke thoroughly approved, as did Tom and Kathie when he told them, out of Spider's hearing, what the proposed gift was to be.

Fate, which was to play a part in the life of Spider Sparrow just as it does in the life of anyone, decreed that, early in 1941, one of the Yorkes' many dogs, an Irish setter, would escape from custody while in heat and make her way down to the village. Here she must have encountered some rustic suitor, identity unknown, for nine weeks later she gave birth to a litter of puppies.

By the time that the broncos had begun to trust Ephraim, the pups were eight weeks old, and one of them, the pick of the litter indeed, was to be offered to Spider. Good red Irish blood they may have had in part, but from the look of things their father had been some sort of hairy Wiltshire cow dog. A day was fixed, a Sunday it was, when Tom and Kathie were to bring their boy along to make his choice.

Spider knew nothing of all this until that morning. Then, at breakfast, his parents decided it best to prepare him for the coming treat.

"Spider," said Tom. "This morning we're going to see Mister. He's got something for you."

"Mister?" said Spider. He took out his knife. "Mister!" he said. "Find knife! Spider give fish!"

"That's right," said Tom.

Busy with the broncos, Spider had not had so much time for carving recently, but he had made one model, his biggest yet, of the Shire mare Flower, for his friend Ephraim.

"Mister's got a present for you," Kathie said.

"For being such a good boy with the broncos," said Tom.

"Good broncos!" said Spider, and he whinnied loudly.

"He's not going to ask what it is," said Kathie. "Should we tell him? We're going to look silly if we get there and he doesn't want one."

"Don't be daft, Kath," said Tom, and they smiled at one another. As instructed, they went not to the house but to the Yorkes' stables, where Mister and his wife met them after church.

Inside, they went along to a stall, at the door of which Mister stopped.

"Spider," he said. "I'm very grateful indeed to you for all the wonderful work you've done with those broncos."

Spider nodded and grinned widely, whinnying

once more, to be answered from their stalls by Sturdiboy and the Yorkes' other two horses.

Mister opened the door. Inside were four droopy-eared, long-tailed, ginger-haired puppies, who came bumbling up, whining and wagging eagerly.

"Lurchers you'd have to call them, I suppose," said Mister to the shepherd, "but they're a nice healthy lot. All four of them are females, but I don't suppose that'll worry the boy. Let him have his pick. Which one d'you fancy, Spider?"

"Pup-pies," Spider said, and he held up four fingers. "Four pup-pies."

"Only one of them is for you," said Tom, and he held up one finger and then pointed it at Spider.

The four adults watched the boy struggling to understand what was happening. He looked at each of them in turn, he looked at the pups, he held up one finger and prodded himself in the chest with it.

"For Spider?" he said. "Pup-py, for Spider?"

"Yes!" they all chorused, watching the play of emotion on his face as the truth of the matter dawned upon him.

"You must choose one," Kathie said. "Which one d'you want?"

In looks the four puppies were very alike. Crossbred they might be, but they all promised to grow into attractive dogs. The only discernible difference in their behavior at this particular moment was that three of them were playing around the feet of the farmer and the shepherd and their wives, jumping up and asking to be petted, while the fourth puppy seemed to have eyes only for Spider. She sat in front of the boy, gazing up at him, and then she gave one little puppy yap. "Pick me," she was saying as plain as could be, and Spider dropped on his knees and took her in his arms and rubbed his cheek against the top of her hairy head.

He looked up at Major Yorke. "Spider's puppy?" he said.

"Yes," said Mister. "For you."

"What d'you say, Spider?" asked Kathie, and when there was no answer, "Aren't you going to say thank you?"

Spider grinned his lopsided grin. "Ta, Mis-ter," he said, and they all laughed.

Back at home, Moss greeted the puppy amiably, but she showed little interest in him. Already it was plain that for her, Spider was the whole world.

As they watched the two of them playing in the garden, Tom said, "What are we going to call her, then?"

"Let Spider choose," said Kathie.

"We'll have to help him. Try some different

names on him. He'll probably pick the first one we say, anyway."

But he didn't. They explained to him that, just as Molly had a name and Moss now had a name, so must his puppy.

"You start, Kath," said Tom.

"How about 'Bess'?" said Kathie, pointing at the pup and looking at Spider. "Bess?"

Spider shook his head.

"'Nell,'" said Tom, but that, too, got a shake and so did half a dozen other suggestions.

"Well," said Kathie, "what d'you want to call her, Spider?"

"Mis-ter," said Spider.

"Aah!" said Kathie. "Because it was a present from him—that's nice, isn't it! But you can't call her that, Spider love. She's got to have a girl's name—you can't call her Mister."

Tom laughed. "You'd have to call her 'Sister,'" he said jokingly.

Spider's face lit up. "Sis-ter!" he said. "Good un! Call Spider's pup-py Sister!"

CHAPTER EIGHTEEN

"HE CAN'T CALL her that!" said Kathie later.

"Don't worry," Tom said. "It'll soon shorten, I'll see to that." And right from the start, he spoke of and to the puppy as "Sis," and Spider soon followed suit.

The summer of 1941 was for Spider the happiest time of his life so far. Not that he knew what year it was, nor would the number have meant anything. When, on his fifteenth birthday, his father held up the fingers and thumb of one hand three times and said, "That's how old you are now," he doubted if the boy could understand.

Spider's happiness was almost wholly due to Sis. Most people have to work, sometimes very hard, at training their dogs, but from an early age Sis seemed to sense what it was that Spider wanted from her.

He had, of course, watched his father working old Molly, and then, later, Moss, and he had picked

up the basic commands, like "Sit" and "Down" and
"Stay" and "Come," nice short words for him to
say, all of whose meanings Sis learned very quickly.
She would come to the whistle, too, the big silver
whistle he used to scare the croaks, but there was
seldom need for this, since she generally stuck to
him like glue. Before she was much older (and
once Kathie was satisfied about house training), Sis
slept on an old rug at the foot of Spider's bed, and
whatever jobs Percy found for him during the
week, she would be sitting or lying near, her eyes
always on him.

"Nothing's never going to surprise me about
young Spider," said Billy to his nephews, "after
what he done with they bleddy horses. Thik dog'll
be walking on its hind legs afore long, I dessay, and
next thing after that, he'll be teaching she to talk.
Not many words, mind you, because the poor
little bagger don't say much hisself, but enough to
say, 'Hullo, Billy' when I do come in stables of a
morning."

"Oh, I don't think she'd say that, Uncle," said
Frank. "She'm a polite sort of dog."

"Frank's right," said Phil. "More likely she'll
say, 'Good morning, Mr. Butt.'"

"Ar, you'm right," said Billy. "'Twould be more
respectful-like."

When the spring corn was drilled, Sis was still very young and merely followed the crowstarver up and down the fields as he banged and yelled and shouted at the black thieves.

But by the time of the autumn drilling, the dog had changed beyond all recognition. Strictly, Mister had been wrong in describing her as a lurcher, for lurchers should have grayhound blood, but nonetheless, she looked like one, long-legged, long-bodied, deep-chested, hard-muscled, and with no hint of superfluous flesh. She looked, in short, like a dog born to run, and run she did as the crowstarver patrolled the winter wheat.

Once she realized—which she very quickly did—that Spider wanted her to chase those flocks of black birds, she extended his territory enormously. For a second year both Maggs' Corner and Slimer's were planted with wheat, but now the croaks could not escape harassment by simply flying from the first to the second, for while slow Spider marched in one, speedy Sis was racing around the other.

The thought that she might catch and kill a bird did not occur to Spider, though it would certainly have worried him if it had. For, as Tom had told him at the very beginning of his crowstarving, he was expected not to hurt the croaks, but just to shout and bang at them.

In fact, despite her speed, there was no chance of her pulling down a crow, a rook, or a jackdaw, for their ultimate safety lay in flight. Other creatures, however, might flee but could not fly, and one day something happened that caused Spider great confusion and distress.

Crossing from one field to the other, boy and dog came out of the spinney—where Spider's house still stood, though now somewhat weather-beaten—to see a host of croaks hard at work. Sis looked at Spider—she would not go until told—and he said, "Good dog!" and pointed at the birds, and away she dashed. Spider walked out toward the opposite end of the field and stood, watching her. Suddenly he saw, not far in front of him, a low brown shape. The hare lay motionless in its form, long ears flat. Big barrit! Spider said to himself, and then he saw Sis, her job done, racing back toward him.

A puff of wind brought the boy's scent sharply to the hare, and it rose and began to lope away. Because of the set of their eyes, hares have poor forward vision, and for a moment this one, looking back, saw the human but not the fast-approaching dog. When it did, it was too late.

It jinked, but before it could gather itself for the high-speed run that the dog could not have matched, Sis swerved and took it across the back. The hare screamed like a child in agony.

"No, Sis, no!" yelled Spider, and he ran toward them in his awkward way, but by the time he reached the hare, it was dead. That afternoon Spider did no more crowstarving. He sat in his house, the body of the hare in his lap, his dog at his feet, whining now and then, for she sensed that something was wrong, though she knew not what.

Spider's thoughts were in a whirl. He had seen death in the animal world before, of course: dead lambs, dead chickens, hedgehogs squashed on the road, naked baby birds fallen from the nest. He knew that Molly had died, though he did not understand how. But this creature, this beautiful "big barrit," had been killed by his own dog, and its screams still rang in his ears. He did not know what to think.

At last, at dusk, he got up and began to make his way home, carrying the hare, the dog at heel.

Kathie was in her kitchen when Spider came in. He laid the body of the hare upon the kitchen table. Then he sat down in a chair, rested his arms on the table, leaned his head upon them, and began to weep. Apart from the time when he was a small baby, Kathie had never seen Spider cry. He might be feeling ill, or be disappointed over something, or have hurt himself in some way, but he never cried.

Tom came in. He looked at the body on the table. He looked at the weeping boy. He looked at the dog lying at the boy's feet, whining softly.

"What's up?" he said to Kathie.

"I don't know. He just came in and put that hare on the table."

"Dog must have killed it," said Tom. He bent and fondled the dog's ears. "Oh, dear, Sis," he said. "Anyone else would have been ever so pleased with you."

He put a hand on Spider's shaking shoulders. "It's all right, son," he said. "It's all right. You don't want to blame yourself, nor Sis, she only done what's natural to a dog." But Spider continued gently to sob.

"You'd best get that thing out of here, Tom," said Kathie. "I want to get things ready for your tea."

"Wass want me to do with it?" said Tom.

"Oh, just get rid of it, bury it, so's he can't see it no more."

Tom took the hare away, and Kathie fetched Spider's new book, which they had given him for his fifteenth birthday. It was another picture book of animals, but this time of exotic ones—lions, tigers, camels, elephants, and so forth—to help him if he should want to try carving some creature that he could not set eyes on in the flesh, and indeed he had made a model of a giraffe.

Now she opened it and put it in front of him. "Have a look at this, Spider love," she said, "while I get your tea."

She wiped his nose and his eyes, and Spider looked up and saw that the table was empty, and his sobs subsided.

"Where big barrit?" he asked, sniffing.

"Dada's gone to bury it," said Kathie.

Gradually, now that he could no longer see the dead animal, Spider began to look less miserable, and the dog, sensing this somehow, put her head on his lap and he stroked it.

Later he had his tea—in silence, but that was usual—and then, as his mother was clearing away the plates, he said to his father, "Sis killed big barrit, Dada."

"I know," said Tom. "'Twasn't your fault, 'twasn't her fault. Next time she goes after one, you blow your whistle and she'll come back."

After Spider was in bed, Sis on her rug at its foot, Kathie said, "What did you do with it?"

"With what?"

"That hare. Did you bury it?"

"Some of it," said Tom.

"What d'you mean?"

"Oh, look, Kath, that was a good big hare, that was. I skinned him and I paunched him, and I buried his skin and his guts, and the rest of him's in the larder. 'Tisn't as though we can afford all that much fresh meat on my wages. You cook him, he'll go down a treat."

"Oh, Tom, but what if Spider should ask what we're eating?"

"He never does, you know that. He just puts down whatever's set in front of him. Apart from his precious licorice allsorts, I don't reckon he ever knows what he's eating."

"But suppose he does ask?"

"Tell him it was chicken."

Tom was right. To Spider, food was simply food, and thoughts of the morality of people killing animals in order to eat them had never crossed his mind.

Kathie was right, too. Had Spider been told that what in due course was set before him was the "big barrit" that Sis had killed, he might well have been terribly upset.

But he didn't ask, he simply cleared his plateful.

Because of that bout of bitter weeping, Tom and Kathie worried that the whole incident might somehow have thrown out of balance the even—if peculiar—tenor of Spider's ways.

But a couple of days later he came home and told them, in his own limited language and by gesture, of something that had obviously made him feel very much happier.

Sis had flushed out another hare and set off in hot pursuit of it, they gathered, and Spider had blown his whistle, and the dog had broken off the chase immediately and come back to him.

"Good Sis!" he had said, and now he said it again, while his dog looked up at him in adoration.

CHAPTER NINETEEN

OVERSEAS, IN DIFFERENT theaters of war, battles were fought and men died, men of Great Britain, Germans, Russians, but life in the village went on quietly and peacefully. Percy Pound's son was dead, to be sure, and Mister's a prisoner, but most other families had not a great deal of which to complain.

They were not in immediate personal danger, they had clothes on their backs and food on their plates—much more than many, for most kept a few hens and grew their own vegetables—and though the news was all of war, day-to-day existence in the Wylye Valley was not greatly different from what it had been in peacetime. Gas was rationed, of course, but few of the villagers had aspired to owning a car, and for most the bicycle, or walking, was an adequate way of getting about.

This is not to belittle the worries that people carried about with them. Victory was assured in the end, they told themselves, but just suppose, they could not help thinking, the Germans won the war? Things didn't seem to be going too well—we'd been driven from Europe, we were getting nowhere in Africa, the Americans were still sitting on the fence.

It was a time when it was difficult to see ahead clearly, and everyone, in some degree, felt fear for the future.

Except Spider.

Despite the shooting down of the Messerschmitt, despite seeing Albie Stanhope on leave in his uniform, despite having been told that Percy's sojer son would never return, Spider had no real concept of the outer world and the cataclysm that was shaking it. Of shortages he knew nothing, he had all that he wanted. Of danger he knew nothing, he could imagine no life except the safe one that he lived, day in, day out, with his mother and father, with Sis and Moss, with his friend Ephraim and the others.

Never in his life had he been to the nearest town, for his world was simply the extent of Outoverdown Farm, bounded at one end by the river Wylye and at the other end by the Far Hanging, away up on the downs.

Within that world there were favorite places: the shepherd's hut, the cart horse stables, his bedroom in the cottage, and his house in the spinney between Maggs' Corner and Slimer's.

He liked to be out in the open, he liked to be by himself, he enjoyed doing his carvings of animals, imitating the calls of animals, exercising the extraordinary hold he had over all creatures.

He was totally unaware of his skills, as indeed he was ignorant of his shortcomings.

In a nutshell, Spider was as unselfconscious as it is possible for a human to be and, having no worries, as happy.

Mister and his wife were saying this, in so many words, as they sat at breakfast one morning.

"I think he was happy before he got his dog," Mister said, "but he's even happier now. Brilliant idea of yours, that was."

"I'd like to think he'll be happy all his life," said Mrs. Yorke. "However long that may be. Now then, I'll have some sandwiches made up. What sort would you like?"

The Yorkes were having a day's hunting. Throughout the war so far, a large landowner, who was a neighbor of theirs and a master of foxhounds, had managed to keep together a scratch pack—a mixed pack of twenty hounds—to give sport for the locals, and for officers on leave from the forces, and of course for the farmers of the district, who provided the kennels with food in the shape of livestock casualties, mainly calves and sheep.

The hounds were meeting at this neighbor's stately home, quite near, a few miles only beyond the southern boundary of Outoverdown Farm, so the Yorkes were hacking to the meet.

"I've told Tom to move his sheep nearer home," Mister said to his wife as they trotted up the drove. "I'm fairly sure those hounds are steady on sheep, but better safe than sorry. It's quite possible a fox might run our way, onto the Far Hanging, say."

After they had disappeared from sight, two figures came out into the drove and followed them: one a tall, thin boy with a strange gait, the other a long-legged, gingery dog.

In the cart horse stables that morning, Percy had given the men their orders while leaning, as always, on Flower's great rump. The Shire mare had long been used to this, and more recently to another attention, for Spider liked to stand at her head while the foreman was talking.

At first he would just croon to her, stroke her muzzle, but then one morning he took from his pocket his usual paper bag of licorice allsorts, put one in his mouth and another on the flat of his hand, and offered it to the mare. She sniffed at it and nuzzled at it with big, soft, rubbery lips. Then she accepted it, and from then on she would each morning nudge Spider with her great head, asking for this odd treat.

She was still mumbling one of the sweets when Percy called, "Spider, come here a minute," and when he did, the foreman said, "You can have the day off today, boy. It's a nice day, and you've worked well this last week, so have a little holiday."

"Hol-i-day!" said Spider. "Ta, Per-cy!"

It was indeed a fine clear winter's day, dry, not too cold—the sort of day, in fact, from a fox hunter's point of view, when scent would lie well.

Spider, Sis at heel, went first for a walk along the bank of the Wylye. Whether or not he remembered his dunking, the river, with its wildlife, was always attractive to him, and there was the chance of a glimpse of the "hotters." He saw none that morning, but sat, Sis still and silent at his side, watching a couple of water voles swimming across, their heads and backs showing above the water, an arrowhead wake trailing from each.

Next he struck across the fields, calling in at his house in the spinney, remembering perhaps the "vox" that had come to take food from his hand, and then he walked along the lynchets that terraced the last slope before the downs. Here were many rabbits, but Sis had now learned that these, like hares, were not for her to chase, and she trotted at her master's heels without affording them so much as a glance.

Meeting the drove at the point where it began to climb steeply, Spider turned up it, continuing his holiday walk and taking his usual pleasure in the peaceful scene and the creatures that inhabited it, while skylark song laced the clear sky above his head, until at last he came to the farthermost gate on the farm, which led to the Far Hanging, a great sweep of downland more than a hundred acres in extent.

Never before had Spider been as far as the southern boundary of this farthest part of the downs, and now he set out across the springy turf toward it. Almost in the center of the Far Hanging was a raised squarish grassy tumulus, a barrow perhaps a hundred yards in length, and in the side of this ancient earthwork were many rabbit holes and, among them, Spider noticed, one much larger hole.

Suddenly he heard a noise in the distance, a noise that he had heard once before, from Slimer's, and had not recognized. This time it was nearer, and though Spider had never in his life set eyes on a foxhound, he knew what kind of animals must be making this noise.

Then he saw a different sort of animal coming over the ridge and making its way toward him.

"Vox!" said Spider softly, and he stood quite still, a hand on Sis's head.

Whether the hunted fox ever focused on the

motionless figure before it is doubtful, so exhausted was it. Its red coat was darkened, its tongue lolled, its ears lay flat, its brush dragged.

All the time the music of hounds grew louder, and now the pack came into Spider's view as they topped the ridge, half a dozen riders not far behind them. The hounds' heads were down as they followed the line, but though still distant, they were making directly for him—for him and Sis.

Spider had no fear for himself, but something, mercifully, told him that, apart from the fox, his reddish-colored dog was also in mortal danger. Thankfully, one of the things that he had taught her was to go home when told, and now he gave the order and away she sped, far faster than any fox-hound could have run.

Before the hunters on horseback streamed the pack, heads up now, for they could see their quarry. Beyond, the exhausted fox dragged itself desperately over the few remaining yards that lay between it and the mouth of its earth in the side of the barrow.

But between the two, hunters and hunted, was running—if you could call such an awkward blunder "running"—the gawky figure of a boy. He was trying, it seemed, to interpose himself between fox and hounds, hounds in full cry and intent on pulling down their fox at the end of a long chase.

Frantically the huntsman galloped, whip cracking, the Yorkes and the others with him, to try to turn the pack before they overran the boy, but in vain.

As the fox crept, with the last of his strength, into safety, so the leaders, but a few yards from his brush, reached Spider, and he tripped and fell, and the rest of the pack flowed over him.

Kathie, bringing in washing from the line behind the cottage, saw Sis come in from the lane. She looked about for Spider but could not see him.

At first Kathie was not especially worried. If anything had happened to Spider—if, say, he had had an accident—the dog would have stayed with him, surely? Oh, but then suppose he had sent her home to fetch help? Was he ill perhaps? He'd never been strong. She put on her coat and hurried out. Not far up the lane she met Ephraim, driving Flower in the big wagon.

"Where's Tom, Eph?" she cried.

"Up in the yard, putting up the lambing pens," he said. "I just come from there, took un up a load of straw."

Kathie hastened up the drove. "Tom," she said when she found him, "I'm worried. Sis came home without Spider. Have you seen him?"

"No," said Tom. "Seen Percy, though. He said he'd given him the day off. He'll have gone for a walk, I dessay."

"But why would he send the dog home?"

Before Tom could answer, they heard the sound of hooves, and, going out into the drove, looked up to see two riders coming down it. It was not until they came nearer that they saw there were in fact three riders, for though Mrs. Yorke's horse carried one burden only, Sturdiboy carried two. Behind Mister, long arms clasped around his scarlet coat, sat Spider.

Tom helped him down, and the Yorkes told them all that had happened.

"We were all absolutely horrified," finished Mister. "He just disappeared under this wave of hounds, hounds with their blood up, that had been within an ace of killing their fox."

"But when we got to him," said Mrs. Yorke, "he was sitting up and the only danger he was in was of being licked to death. Every single hound in the pack seemed to want to wash his face, his hands, any bit of him they could lay a tongue on."

"He had his arms around a big hound, Gambler it was," said Mister, "and it was wagging its tail off. 'Bad dog,' he was saying to it."

"Oh, Spider!" cried Kathie. "Are you all right?"

Spider nodded. Then he said, "Bad dogs. Mustn't hurt vox."

"If it had been any other boy," said Mister, "I dread to think what might have happened."

"He's not like any other boy, sir," said Tom. "Thank God."

CHAPTER TWENTY

AT THE TIME of Spider's sixteenth birthday, in 1942, Tom did not get much help from him during lambing season, for the crowstarver was too busy at his first job. Mister was plowing up larger and larger acreages of downland to grow more wheat and barley and oats for the war effort (and for his own profit—farmers have no objection to making money). Maggs' Corner had been re-seeded to a three-year ley—a temporary pasture—but Slimer's had been drilled with spring barley and the croaks were as predatory as ever.

A cold wet spell in April meant that after each attack against the robbers, Spider was glad to seek refuge in his house.

One day he had marched to the far end of Slimer's, banging his old sheet of tin, blowing his whistle, and shouting "Ee-orr!" and "Oo-ah! Oo-ah!" Then he noticed a movement under the hedge at the top of the field and saw there a partridge with a brood of nine or ten little chicks. It was coming on to rain hard, and the mother bird was trying to shield her babies from the weather as it rapidly worsened. There was a sudden flash of lightning, followed almost immediately by a rumble of thunder, and then the heavens opened and the rain came down in great sheets.

For a moment Spider stood there, wondering what he could do for the hen partridge and her brood, and then, already soaked, he hurried back to the spinney and the shelter of his house. The storm continued for some while, as Spider sat on his wooden crate in his sodden clothes, Sis shivering beside him. He was as wet as if he had once more fallen in the Wylye, but when the rain relented, he saw the croaks returning.

Anyone else would have left them to their devices and gone off to change into dry clothing, but Spider took up his duties again, drenched as he was.

By the time he reached home that evening he was shuddering with the cold and the wet, and Kathie hastened to put the old copper hip bath in front of the fire and fill it with kettles full of hot water.

The next morning Spider had a nasty cough, and, Kathie suspected, on feeling his forehead, a temperature.

"I'm not taking him to the doctor's in this weather," she said to Tom, for it was still cold and very wet. "The doctor will have to come here. You go down and see Percy" (the foreman had a telephone), "and ask him will he ring up?"

When the doctor came, he took Spider's temperature and sounded his narrow chest. He spent some little time listening through his stethoscope.

"He's got a chill, Mrs. Sparrow," he said. "Keep him in bed. I'll leave you some medicines, and I'll look in tomorrow."

Standing poking the fire that evening, Kathie suddenly turned to her husband. "What's to become of him, Tom?"

"Don't fret, Kath love," Tom said. "It's nothing much, he'll soon be better."

"No, I mean what's to become of him when we're gone?"

"Dead, you mean?"

"Yes. How will he ever manage on his own?"

Tom got out of his chair and put his arms around his wife. "Come on now, love," he said. "We're not that old!"

Tom was at home when the doctor next came and again listened carefully to Spider's chest. Then he said, "Good-bye, John Joseph" (at which Spider looked completely blank), and went downstairs.

"I don't think you've a lot to worry about," he said to Tom and Kathie. "Like I said, it's just a chill."

"He's not coughing so much today, Doctor," said Kathie.

"Good. His temperature's down a bit."

"He's never been ill in his life before," Tom said. "Bit short of breath sometimes, but never what you'd call ill."

"Is that so?" said the doctor. He had not been long in the district and had not met the Sparrows before, though he had, of course, at once realized that Spider was slow. He was a young man but yet an old-fashioned sort of a doctor, who believed among other things that it was always best to call a spade a spade, and so tried not to sugarcoat his pills. He also thought that it was the job of the head of any household to take what knocks might threaten his family. Had he been a ship's doctor, he would have expected every man, in the face of disaster, to cry, "Women and children first!"

Accordingly now, having said his good-byes to Kathie along with certain admonishments as to Spider's treatment, he lured Tom to walk out with him by admiring the beauty of the cabbages in his garden.

Then, when they reached his car, the doctor

said, "I think it best that you should know, Mr. Sparrow, that your boy has a slight heart problem. I didn't want to worry your wife with it, but I have to tell you that he has what we call a heart murmur. I could hear it quite plainly through my stethoscope—it's an abnormal rustling sound, quite unmistakable."

"Dear God!" said Tom. "He's abnormal enough as 'tis, poor lad."

"It may be nothing to concern yourself about," said the doctor, "but I thought it right to tell you. If he should show any symptoms of heart trouble in the future, we can have a much more thorough look at him. I shouldn't worry your wife about it."

"What was he on about?" asked Kathie when the doctor had driven away.

"Oh, just chatting," said Tom.

Thus it was that the shepherd, who had saved the life of the infant Spider sixteen years earlier, was now the only one to know that that life might possibly be threatened.

Spider did not know, of course, nor Kathie, nor Mister and his wife, nor Percy, nor any of those who worked on Outoverdown Farm. Only Tom knew and only Tom worried, and even he, as haymaking passed and harvesttime came and went, and Spider appeared in every way his usual self, began to be less concerned. Some days he never even thought about it.

It was a wonderful summer for Spider. Early on, at the end of May, he stumbled upon a litter of fox cubs. There was an earth, part hidden by a stunted sentinel thornbush, in one of the banks of the lynchets, and one day Spider saw from a distance the cubs come out to play.

From then on he would go to see them whenever he could, gradually approaching nearer. Often the vixen scented and saw the silent watcher but seemed not to mind.

Spider would leave Sis at home on these occasions, telling her (in front of Kathie, so that she, too, would understand), "Spider go see baby voxes." Then he would walk up to the lynchets and sit and look down at the cubs, their coats still woolly and gray-brown, their tails small and pointed, playing tag, mock-fighting, scratching their fleas, and occasionally looking, bright-eyed and fearless, up at him.

There were "hotters" to watch, too. The female in the willow tree holt had given birth to three cubs in the spring, and Spider quite often saw the four of them—the male otter, as was usual, had gone away elsewhere—in the daytime. Most otters sleep the day away inside their holts, but this family seemed to come out on purpose to greet Spider.

One evening he saw, in the spinney, an animal he'd never before set eyes on. It was a thickset bear-like animal that walked with a slow rolling shuffle, head and tail low. When it saw Spider, it did not flee but stood and stared at him, and then made a clucking sound of pleasure before passing him unconcernedly by. Spider soon found its picture in his old book, and Kathie told him its name.

"Budger!" said Spider, smiling, and he clucked at her.

Earlier in the year, a pair of house martins had built their nest, a half-cup made of mud, under the cottage eaves; it was but a few feet from his bedroom window, and once the eggs were hatched, he could lean out and look up and watch the parents bringing insects for the four hatchlings, both birds in no way disturbed by his nearness.

All creatures allowed him near—"barrits," "big barrits," partridges, pigeons—any and every animal he met. It was as though all the wildlife of Outoverdown Farm wanted to make the summer of 1942 a very special one for Spider Sparrow.

It was not only the wild animals that gave him pleasure, of course. There were the cattle and sheep, always glad to have him move among them, and Flower and his other friends in the cart horse stable, and, especially perhaps, the six once-wild broncos.

These were now fit to be sold as riding horses, said Mister, and he had every intention of selling them, he told his wife. But somehow the months passed and still the four pintos, the sorrel, and the buckskin continued to enjoy their freedom on the downs and, when possible, the company of Spider.

So summer prepared to give way to autumn, and Tom had almost completely forgotten the doctor's visit and his words of warning. Then came one peerless day in late September, a Sunday it was, when the sun still shone warmly from an almost cloudless blue sky, and the breeze was gentle, and the Wylye Valley at its most beautiful. It was a day when, here on the wide Wiltshire downs, it did not seem possible to believe in the war, with its daily bulletin of death.

That afternoon Spider made it plain that he was going for a walk.

"Not too far, mind," said Kath, "and you be back in good time for your tea. I got a nice piece of meat for you and your father."

"What time, Mum?" asked Spider, turning his wrist to look at the watch they had bought him for his sixteenth birthday present. It was a cheap one, they couldn't afford better, but it kept good time, which Spider had learned to tell, with practice. He knew what it meant when the long hand pointed straight up, and Tom had taught him to count around the dial to tell what hour it was.

Now Tom said, "I got a sick ewe up in the yard as I want to take a look at later. You meet me there, Spider, and we'll walk home together. You be there, at my hut, five o'clock, all right?" And he held up four fingers and a thumb.

They watched him set off up the road with that distinctive walk, his watch on his wrist, his knife in his pocket, his dog at heel.

"He's happy, our boy, isn't he, Tom," Kathie said. It was a statement, not a question.

"Long may he be so," said Tom.

When five o'clock came, Tom was in the shepherd's hut doing some odd jobs while he waited for his son, but time passed without sight of him. Tom went outside the yard and looked around the fields but could not see him coming. He misunderstood, Tom thought, he'll have made his own way home. But then he heard in the distance the noise of a dog howling. It seemed to be coming from the direction of the spinney. "Come, Moss," said Tom, and he set off across the grass ground that led to both Maggs' Corner and Slimer's.

That's got to be Sis howling, he thought. Why? What happened? He quickened his steps toward the spinney. Now he could see that its greenness was stippled with black, for in every ash tree there sat crows and rooks and jackdaws, still and silent.

"Spider!" called Tom, and at the sound of his voice the howling stopped, and the birds rose in a great flock.

Sis was sitting outside Spider's house. She ran to him as he approached and then ran back again. Tom followed, running too now.

"Spider?" he said again as he reached the over-grown shelter, but there was no answer. Tom bent to look inside.

Spider was sitting on the wooden crate, his back against the hurdle wall, his long arms hanging by his sides. His eyes were closed. He looked to be fast asleep.

Tom took hold of Spider's hand. It was cold. He felt for a pulse. There was no pulse. That heart, that murmuring heart, was still. Now the shepherd carried the boy slung across his shoulders, as he would have carried a dead ewe, back over the grass field to the yard, the two dogs following.

High above them, the croaks, silent still, caprioled and curvetted in the sky, an aerial ballet bidding a final farewell to the crowstarver.

Tom opened the door of the shepherd's hut, so close to which he had first set eyes on the foundling, and laid Spider gently on the rough wooden bunk. Moss sat silent, but Sis crept forward, whining softly, and licked at one cold hanging hand.

"It's all right, girl," Tom said softly. "We'll look after you." He stood gazing down upon the face of this, his only son. It wore its customary lopsided smile.

"He's happy," said Tom to the watching dogs. "Thank God, he's happy."

ABOUT THE AUTHOR

DICK KING-SMITH was born and raised in Gloucestershire, England. He served in the Grenadier Guards during World War II, then returned home to Gloucestershire to realize his lifelong ambition of farming. After twenty years as a farmer, he turned to teaching and then to writing the children's books that have earned him many fans on both sides of the Atlantic. Inspiration for his writing has come from his farm and his animals.

Among his well-loved novels for younger readers are *Babe: The Gallant Pig*, *Three Terrible Trins*, *Harriet's Hare*, and *A Mouse Called Wolf*. In 1992, he was named Children's Author of the Year at the British Book Awards. In 1995, *Babe: The Gallant Pig* became a critically acclaimed major motion picture that was later nominated for an Academy Award.